ASTRIDE

TALES OF THE ARGENTINE DIASPORA

RAFAEL PINTOS-LÓPEZ

To all young Argentinians who unfortunately feel they have to leave the country. Do not worry. Argentina lives within you.

EPIGRAPH

None of us are getting out of here alive... Say the truth that you're carrying in your heart like hidden treasure. Be silly. Be kind. Be weird. There's no time for anything else.

Anthony Hopkins

CONTENTS

INTRODUCTION

After 53 years in Australia, I thought it was time to put these short stories into writing. Some are semi-autobiographical, or, as the Japanese would call them, *watashi no monogatari* (私の物語, tales of mine), some are pure fiction, and some segments are there to give context to the short stories. The titles of the latter are marked with an asterisk.

Human migration is a natural phenomenon, as walking is. It has happened since the dawn of humanity, when groups of *Homo Sapiens* left Africa and commenced wandering the planet. The subtitle of this book includes the word *'diaspora'*, which involves the concept of migration, but *'diaspora'* is a more specific term. It is a Greek word used to describe a scattered population who identify with a homeland where they cannot live. And many of us cannot live in Argentina any longer. It has become a different country from the country we grew up in.

By the time I left, Peronism, greedy politicians and soldiers, decades of corruption and weak democratic institutions had turned Argentina—which was among the richest countries in the world—into a desert. Young people desperate for a future began to leave in droves. That period marked the start of the exodus of the hundreds of thousands of Argentinians who have left and now live abroad. Things have not improved. On the contrary, with a new populist/leftist brand of Peronism, things have got far worse. And the exodus continues.

Whether one wants to explain the experience in the diaspora, give a context to the short stories that follow, or provide the perspective of an Argentinian, there is no escape from self-referencing. A famous American actor said he loved stories that were dark, strange, and weirdly personal (or words to that effect). Well, I believe these stories fit that description. Elsewhere in this book I say that talking about oneself is never good. I apologise, then, for falling into this trap. In any case, I feel I must tell you briefly how this diaspora thing began.

WHAT LEAVING WAS LIKE *

*"And she bare him a sonne, and he
called his name *Gershom: for he said,
I haue been a stranger in a strange land"*
– Exodus 2:22

Who said that part of being an Argentinian was leaving the country? Truth is I don't remember. Actually, it doesn't matter. Leaving was hard. Coming to Australia felt good, though. Australia is probably the best country in the world now. And from the very beginning it was like a mother that received us with open arms. Here, it's easy to feel that one belongs. However, I have to admit, one remains an Argentinian even after such a long time.

As I was explaining, what happened to me happened to many other South Americans: there had been a military coup. The year was 1966. General Onganía had deposed President Illia. Things had deteriorated to such a point that survival with a young family was extremely difficult. By 1968 I felt there was no alternative. I had to leave.

At that point in time, Australia needed migrants. When my mate Ernesto and I applied, getting a permanent resident visa was much easier than now. There were no queues.

Paying for the trip was not as easy. Funds were limited. I had my meagre redundancy payment from work. Mum sold two of her paintings that she loved and gave me the money.

The plan was that we had to catch a ship of the 'Compagnie des Messageries Maritimes' that was leaving from the Panama Canal on 10 May 1968 (so long ago!). We couldn't get enough money for airfares all the way to Australia. I paid for the boat from Panama. Ernesto could get to two tickets on a LADE flight to Quito (LADE was the State-run airline). That was going to be his contribution to the trip. Reaching Panama from Quito would be easy, we hoped.

The worst part was seeing mum and waving goodbye as the lift went down from her flat. She was as sad as I was, but she really wanted me to come to Australia. What neither of us knew was that we would not see each other again.

We left with Ernesto on the LADE flight, with two suitcases full of hopes and many fears I never confess. Before Quito there was a stopover in Lima for one day and one night.

We didn't have any money for a hotel so, as soon as we arrived, we went out for a walk around Lima and spent most of the day getting to know the place. As soon as it got dark we went back to the airport to spend the night sleeping on the seats there (at the time, Jorge Chávez Airport had beautiful, very comfortable, leather armchairs). We boarded the plane again and we reached Quito. Then I realised that there was no going back. We had crossed the Rubicon.

We discovered we could not cross Colombia hitch-hiking— which, stupidly, was our original plan— as the country was in the middle of a war between guerrillas / drug traffickers and the government. We eventually caught a plane to Panama. Our meagre resources became almost non-existent.

Coming out of the Canal through Panama City into the Pacific was an unforgettable experience. It was getting dark and the Ocean was enormous. I thought of Vasco Núñez de Balboa, the *conquistador* who first crossed the Isthmus of Panama. But we were going much, much farther away. The Pacific, like the pampa, was wide and unknown to us. It ended up being much wider and much more beautiful than we had imagined.

There were many days with no land in sight. I discovered that sometimes the Pacific could be as calm as a lake. It is like a mirror as far as your eyes can see. Some other times, there were schools of tuna or dolphins jumping around. And at night, you could often see luminous masses of fish.

As we arrived in Nuku Hiva, capital of the Marquesas, many Polynesian men and women came rowing in their canoes to say hello. The ship would normally anchor say a hundred meters from the shore. The Marquesans came aboard and some of them would dance while some others would stretch their tapa blankets on deck and display their merchandise for sale. We didn't realise it then, but we were witnessing something that is history now. As far as I know they don't do it anymore anywhere in the Pacific. We were amazed at the sound of their language.

Afterwards we spent five days in Papeete, Tahiti, where beautiful *vahines* would zoom around in their scooters, their long black hair in the wind; the huge yachts of the millionaires would be on exhibition for you to envy, and flowers would grow even in the gutters.

Papeete was much smaller in those days. Most houses and shops were weatherboard. All of the shop owners were Chinese and spoke broken French and very little English. We passed Tonga and stopped over in Noumea, New Caledonia, and Port Vila, in what was then the New Hebrides.

The weather had become cooler and we arrived in Sydney on 10 June 1968. I remember quite distinctly entering Sydney Harbour and going under the bridge. By then it was really cold. After a month in Polynesia, we had one dollar between the two of us. The Argentine Consul, who had gone to welcome the few Argentinians on the boat, told us, especially Ernesto and me: "Kids, go back home. This place is a shit hole". Luckily, we didn't have the means and couldn't have left even if we had wanted to.

From Sydney we had to hitch-hike to Canberra (two hundred and fifty kms). As it was getting darker, near Goulburn, we thought we had to sleep in the open. Luckily, even though it was really dark, a military guy coming back from Viet Nam picked us up. He needed to chat with somebody to stay awake. Of course, I chatted while Ernesto slept in the back seat because he had no clue of what was going on. I can't remember a word that guy said. I was really, really tired. That had been the beginning of the adventure.

Finding a job in Canberra was easy then. I got an interview the first week and started working as a postman, then we both worked as builder's labourers, and for a few months as printer's assistants, cleaning huge printing machines. Then Ernesto went to work in the Snowy Mountains Hydroelectric Scheme. I got a job in a library.

Coda

The other day, talking to Ernesto, he reminded me of a story that I had forgotten. When we were spending the night at Lima Airport, waiting and trying to sleep, a boy who must have been about ten years old approached us. He was a shoeshine boy. He talked to Ernesto.

"Do I shine your shoes, Sir?"

Ernesto, very politely, told him:

"Look, little boy, we have no money. We are very poor and we are going very far away, to a place on the other side of the Pacific Ocean. We don't know if we're going to have enough money to get there."

The kid was amazed to see that there were two travellers who were so poor that they couldn't have their shoes shined. Especially because we were white, European-looking. Like most shoeshine boys in South America, he was of Indian extraction. He stared at us, he studied us for a short while, and then he left.

About half an hour later he came back with eight or nine shoeshine boys like him, who stared at us in disbelief.

Without saying a word, the boy approached Ernesto, grabbed his hand and put a fistful of coins he had collected among his friends. Then they all left in silence.

We were both frozen. The moment touched us deeply.

Three human beings had met at a transit point. One of them had a beautiful gesture. It was something we couldn't have expected. He knew he was not going to see us again, ever, and —poor as he was— this little boy had the incredible generosity of collecting money to give us. A legend. I'm sure he has been very successful in his life. At least I wish that with all my heart.

BUDDHA

To my friend Enrique.
You know who you are.

I remembered him many of those empty, lonely, days. Many Sundays when you finish a book and—still in robe at noon—check if there's something still edible in the fridge.

We'd been good friends but, strangely, I had lost track of him.

There had been many jobs and girlfriends and houses. In my case, even a couple of marriages. Many years had passed without the slightest piece of news from him. Now I had found out he was OK. Well, more than OK.

The person I saw during my visit was the same person he always was. And yet, he had become somebody else. I know.

Even now I find it hard to believe, maybe because we were good friends for such a long time.

~

THE BEGINNING of our friendship was unremarkable. I remember winter had just started. It was beautiful to see people with thick, warm jackets and coats. It gave you a certain feeling of contentedness, of prosperity. Those days you could feel that everyone in Canberra was doing something, everyone appeared to share a plan. Somehow, the scene comes to my mind with intense colours, not the same colours I see nowadays. They possibly were: it was nineteen sixty-nine and we were all a bit hippy. Some of us weren't aware that was the case.

A young couple with babies, Celia and I were busy gathering twigs and feathers for our nest. We had gone to Civic (that's what you called the CBD in Canberra) to buy a TV set which, of course, we were probably going to pay over three years. I remember we were leaving J B Young's carrying a big carton with the TV set, when we saw him for the first time. Actually, he approached us:

"Excuse me, you're from Argentina, aren't you?"—the question was a bit hard to understand: one, because there was an incredible racket all around us; two, because his English had a very strong South American accent, not from any part of South America, mind you, but from Salta, in Argentina (the accent does exist, but it's not something you hear every day); and three, because his voice had a bit of a tremor to it. You could hear that he was trying really hard, he had to overcome his natural shyness to talk to us. Everything in Enrique was plain and unassuming, even his brown, curly hair. Had he been wearing a hat and braces, he could have been Amish. Somehow you could feel there was something wholesome, something kind of rural about him. He was a few years younger than us, so we saw him as a kid. I remember he was wearing a blue jacket, an army disposals shirt and a pair of jeans.

"Beg your pardon?" —said Celia, who was a bit hard of hearing at the best of times.

"No, I asked if you were from Argentina. I overheard you speaking Spanish as you were passing by, and that accent from Buenos Aires sounded like a flag fluttering in the wind. It is a bit like that, don't you think?".

We loved the compliment. "Bordering on the lyric"— said Celia in the car. I thought it was kind of weak, beginning in "no", as if excusing himself for speaking, and then finishing in "don't you think?", asking for approval. "Young and no self-assurance", I thought.

New to Canberra, Celia and I had very few friends. In any case, we asked him to come to our place a couple of hours later for a cup of coffee. He turned up a few minutes early. Celia brought some mugs with steaming coffee and we started chatting about a thousand different things. Enrique was hungry for company, as were we. Becoming friends wasn't difficult. Of course, there were all the things that Argentinians have in common, especially in the diaspora. But there was much more than that, he was fairly well-read for his age. In those days it wasn't so strange for a young Argentinian to know about the Beatniks. He had read Kerouac. But he also knew details about Corso and Ferlinghetti for instance. He enjoyed his literature. That evening we went from *Howl* to Herman Hesse in a few minutes. And it didn't stop there. At about half past three in the morning we had no more coffee, no cigarettes, and we didn't have a lot of *yerba maté* left either. By five o'clock we had reached Cortázar. Even when he was much younger than us, Enrique was the kind of person we would have had as a friend in Buenos Aires.

We kept on seeing each other. Many, many times. My friendship with him got stronger through countless cups of coffee and outings, and moving houses, and trips, and projects together. Of course, we talked about literature again, and many other subjects. We talked about religion and philosophy. He was very interested in Zen Buddhism.

"What fascinates me about the Beat Generation,"—he used to tell me, drawing slowly from a bamboo bong he had made himself—"is how they mixed seamlessly with junkies and hobos. No barriers. A world of adults without rules or family or responsibilities. An almost wild experience. Kind of making friends with wolves. Maybe living a true life is doing that, if there is any fucking truth at all".

Encouraging his naïve imagination, in a conceited sort of way, I used to tell him anecdotes of a cousin of mine, of a well-to-do family, who, every eighteen months or so, would go on trips as a hobo, not hitch-hiking like kids nowadays, but as a real drifter. He would disappear, busk and beg, live for months without a penny, like the lilies of the field, and then he would return home, filthy and tired. His family knew they couldn't ask any questions. As time passed, he would start opening up and, every now and then—after lunch sometimes—stories of trips and adventures would come to light.

Enrique and I knew that many authors had written about the subject. That was not a coincidence. Definitely, there was a line that went, for instance, from the surrealism of Horacio

Oliveira's famous experience with the *clochards*, to Zen Buddhism. Where was the path? Enrique would laugh at me because I had learnt some Japanese hoping Suzuki would make more sense. That was a crazy dream. In any case, I would still go to an office to work every day. How could you reconcile the word 'satori' with the word 'journalist'?

The sixties were a time of search in the West. Young people wanted to reach that spiritual something that you could not find here. Many went to India. Many went to Tibet and Japan. Perhaps living here was comfortable but not conducive to wisdom, to happiness, to contentment?

Dope and induced hallucinations would give you a fleeting illusion of it. The Beatles were looking for it. For a moment it seemed that mushrooms, Ravi Shankar and Santana would take you there. As far as I was concerned, no Westerner had heard the sound of one hand clapping.

"You are a walking oxymoron, man"—Enrique would tell me with his voice from Salta— "where can you find a Zen journalist? No such thing. You have to give up and start again."

"Unfortunately, I can't turn back time. The only thing I can do is approach the thing from wherever I am. Fate takes people to different places. There are monks that do the same thing every day all their lives to reach enlightenment. And then there are guys who achieve the same result overnight. But there are many paths to *satori*."—I would try to reply, a bit upset.

"Well, you think it's absurd for Siddharta to end up being a boatman. What would be absurd would be for him to be anything else, can't you see? No managers, or MPs, or university professors have ever been there. Not to my knowledge, anyway. It's not a West vs East thing, as you think. Some ancient Greeks were kind of close, don't forget old Diogenes living in his barrel, he must have been a cool dude that one. If it is a matter of class or politics, remember that the left is always closer to the truth."

There was a bit of finger-pointing in his voice, and he was accusing me of being a bit of a fuddy-duddy. He was telling me that if you wanted to go anywhere you had to start walking, and there were no limits that could stop you

Approximately one year later, Enrique went to Europe on his version of the *Grand Tour*.

Letters and postcards would arrive from the ship. Photos from South Africa, then long letters from Germany and France. The trip ended up being a literary pilgrimage. Enrique would send newspaper clippings, cards, bits of paper he would have at hand, from the *Café des Deux-Magots* and places like that. After a few months, the letters started thinning out. There was one from Kensington, and after that, nothing. There was no way to get in touch with him. He would move from one place to the other, and by the time we received an address he would have left.

Two years passed. At some point, somebody said Enrique was coming back, so I found out the date and flight number and went to the airport to wait for him. When he stepped off the plane not even his family recognised him. From what we could see, there had been a big change: he had a huge— massive—afro, a beard, silver boots up to his knees, a very short jacket and a short red cape. He wore beads all over the place, and I'm sure the smell of *patchouli* must have been pretty unbearable to the poor hostesses. He smelled as if he had marinated in it.

As I was telling you, being young is searching. Enrique's search had crossed the tangent of hippiedom in a squat in London. He had found an identity he felt comfortable in. Perhaps it had not been made to measure for him, but it was close.

The change in appearance was complete. The ideas were the same, but you could tell they had been refined to some extent. Until then, the idea that Enrique was focussed, (or obsessed, some would have risked) had not occurred to me. The big change that was so noticeable after the trip to Europe was more than superficial: Enrique had a plan and he was applying it to his life.

We went back to the long chats with big mugs of coffee and Buddha sticks. We went back to literature and Zen. The only difference was that Enrique's lifestyle was based on an alternative I didn't fully understand. Before, the difference in our ages had given me the possibility of telling him about my experiences, of kind of providing advice like an uncle would. Now, it was very difficult for me to give advice on life to someone who had spent six months in a rehab farm near London. Enrique had never done hard drugs, but he had squatted with these people because he had friends who were junkies, because it cost nothing and because he had learnt to accept things like morphine, methadone and petty crime in a way that I could not accept.

One day we went fishing to Scrivener Dam, which is a quiet place. Excellent for trout. Enrique used to be good at fishing. Every now and then he would have vegan scruples, though. I would tease him no end. I can still remember him that day, trying to untangle a line. He turned around and said:

"Have you realised, man, that people like Jesus, and Lao Tzu, used to speak in parables and similes and things of that sort? In a way that's what Japanese monks do with their *koan*. Do you think our Western logic distorts so much? Are we so stupid that they have to draw things for us to understand them?" —Enrique was chatting with me, but he was actually asking himself those questions aloud.

"You have no idea what's going on around you. You're stoned all day. No, seriously, I imagine they did it because there was no other way. It's like wanting to explain to a mouse what goes on in the mind of a human being, more or less. Look, I'm sure that having reached *satori* means to understand why today, for instance, I thought of a winter morning in *Playa Grande* while I was shaving, or why…".

"Yes, that too, but there are physical and physiological explanations for that. It's like *déjà vu*. What's important is to understand that what sometimes seems absurd also makes sense. The sound of the tree falling in the forest and things like that. What's important is entering that illogical life, if you know what I mean, to be able to run away from all this Aristotelian shit that we are fed since childhood. Understanding means being free. That would be marvelous, wouldn't it? I can almost feel what it would be like."

The housing commission house he went to live in was fairly old. It had been built probably around nineteen-thirty or so. It had been abandoned and a hippy commune had happily squatted in it. That time comes back to my mind as through a thick fog. Apart from the *papier mâché* tree in the middle of the living room, the clearest image is that of the interior walls, almost non-existent, eaten away by huge holes the size of doors. Hippies would wander around that almost open-space house with their dope and their art and colourful crafts. Enrique and his girlfriend shared a bunk upstairs.

One year later, somebody brought news to the commune. It was about Bhagwan.

It didn't take long for Enrique to get into the doctrine boots and all.

I could not understand so much dedication to something. So much devotion to that obscure doctrine that ended up being a ruse, a scheme, of that false *"guru"*. In Enrique's case, it was as if those aims had grown from inside the body and had extended to his clothes. Ah, my binary mind. In those days I didn't understand that there were many realities. To me things were either black or white; there were truths and lies.

I kept in contact with him for a couple of years. He was always dressed in orange, with beads and a portrait of Bhagwan hanging from his neck. We kept on chatting about the same old things, but our spontaneity had disappeared. To me, it was like being friends with a priest, although the situation was very different.

I heard that he went with his wife to an *Ashram* in Poona, India. The following year, another hippy told me she had seen him in a farm Bhagwan had in Oregon. After that, there were many years of silence.

LAST CHRISTMAS, a friend who works for the Sydney Morning Herald offered me a project in L.A. It was in collaboration with the Los Angeles Times. We had to discuss the experience of Latinos in Australia and compare it with the Chicano community in California. Very interesting. Of course, I accepted straight away. No hesitation whatsoever.

Celia and I had been divorced a long time. My boys were already grown-up men. I could travel on assignment on one day's notice without having to think about any major responsibilities: nobody would be waiting for me with dinner in the oven.

Convincing Jenny, the neighbour, to feed Sweetie and collect the mail from my letterbox for a few days was a real cinch. As soon as those details were taken care of, the only thing left was putting my clothes in the suitcase.

The Serepax my colleague and I took on departure worked wonders. It was a long snooze interrupted by meals, and then we arrived around noon, well rested and without any jetlag. After leaving our luggage in one of those motels around the airport, we hurried towards East L.A. to interview two famous Chicanos who, incidentally, were really friendly, nice people. We didn't have a lot of time, so social niceties were fairly limited during the trip.

Luckily, I had a few moments to do small talk with one of the two celebrities we had to interview, a Mexican painter who would produce huge murals in fairly organic greenish hues. We talked about Catholicism and processions, about the colours and the beautiful expressions in the faces of the people during those events. She agreed with me that in places like Mexico and Andalusia, processions were incredibly traditional and that there was a lot of devout feeling to them. More than anywhere else in the world, she thought. I agreed:

"I have seen the fervour Sevillans show during Easter. Shame the tradition was not kept in Argentina, or at least not in

Buenos Aires. I imagine in places like Salta or other northern provinces of Argentina, processions are still very traditional. That is part of being Latin American, or Hispanic, as *Gringos* like to call us here in L.A."

"Hey, funny you mention that: a couple of days ago I was talking to a friend of mine, from Salta, who wants to convince me to go there to paint the faces of people from that province. He also lived in Australia, so maybe you know him..."

At that point I wanted to explain that that's the sort of thing that happens when we're overseas: people would say "—Ahh, I have a friend whose name is Jacob and he lives in Perth, maybe you know him.": actually Australia is almost as large as the United States or Brazil, and has a population of almost twenty-six million. I was about to say that, but before I had time to open my mouth.

"His name is Enrique González-Lucca" —she smiled when she noticed my amazement at how small the world had become. Of course, I immediately asked for his phone number and address to go see him.

Usually, evenings in the States make me feel kind of lonely, or humble. I don't know, a bit like being on a ship at night in the middle of the ocean. One feels tiny. Probably in the States it has to do with how massive everything is. Doesn't matter who you're with or what you're doing. Especially in Los Angeles. Especially during the Christmas holiday.

The afternoon was coolish. The taxi driver—a chatty black guy, who probably took me on a drive much longer than needed—explained how his brother-in-law, an electrician with Otis, had got a promotion *"Cuz, man, can he talk"*. When we arrived at the address, right at the farther end of Annaheim, the cottage was L.A. suburban, middle class and fairly plain.

Enrique was waiting in the garden, one arm over Lupita's shoulder. While the taxi was getting in the driveway, they were discussing a myrtle. How you prune a myrtle. She was a high-cheek-boned Latin beauty, bosomy, smiling. Her jet-black hair was tied in one plait. He, in his usual dungarees, looked slightly bigger than I remembered. His curls had gone totally grey.

As only happens with good friends, it was like seeing each other after a couple of days. Enrique's laughter thundered all around the house.

Lupe also laughed, kind of unwittingly, and her laughter had a magical effect. It illuminated her surroundings. The whole thing was contagious. And I'm sure she barely understood why the anecdotes were funny.

After a dinner that was perhaps too Mexican for my taste, but nice, Enrique and I sat a little while longer with two enormous mugs of coffee, while Lupe ironed, at a distance, entranced in her world.

"And so...? "—I looked up. The question was brief, but he knew it was encompassing.

"Look, carpentry was always my thing. Also, here in California you cannot be but comfortable." Enrique was eluding the question with a small answer.

"Yeah, but why L.A.? Why carpenter? How did you decide you wanted to do this? And is this what you want to do?"

"Ahhh... "—his face changed. It looked kind of distant— "Why not? Well, this question has many answers. In any case, having one answer isn't important. Wherever I am, whatever I do, I will be happy, I know. Anyway, let me tell you a story, in Jakarta I met this Dutch guy who was colour-blind. His name was Wilheim. Poor guy, he could only see black and white. Can you imagine? All his life, seeing things in black and white, what a curse that must be. The thing is that one day, talking about something unrelated and trivial, he told me that, once, he had seen colours. It had happened suddenly, coming back from a soccer match in Surabaya. Told me it was like an explosion. Didn't know why. He stopped the car and looked around. What he saw was the most beautiful picture he had seen in his life. Everything was in technicolor. He saw the pink hues of his skin, the brown shoes he was wearing, the details in a magazine he had left on the seat next to him. He saw how green the plants around him were, the gray road with greenish reflections in the distance. He discovered that his car was a very deep maroon. He saw shades and tones. (When Willy was telling me this I imagined something unreal and fantastic. Fiction becoming reality and vice versa. But the experience, in real life, is not like *Don Juan's*, the one in the story by Castañeda. Nothing to do with Saint Joseph of Cupertino, levitating in church). Unfortunately, poor Willy had that kind of vision for about fifteen minutes. I felt sorry for him. But what is interesting is when you can see the colours and the change is permanent."

What Enrique was telling me was a parable and a metaphor. And he knew it had taken me by surprise and I was trying to grasp the whole meaning.

"I don't think I'm following all this." —the anxiety in my question changed the pitch of my voice.

"There are ways and ways people can understand things. Many people cannot accept that everything fluctuates, that everything changes. I know, in minute detail, how you and I are the same person. But there is no mysticism, no sophistication. I just know it."—the smile, which had returned to his lips, became loud laughter.

"Hey, Enrique," I said— the parable becoming increasingly clearer—"I am the one who could not understand how Siddharta could be a boatman."

"Ahh" he said—"but then you were young, and the Gates of Wisdom are rarely open to the young, as you very well know. There is a path, and there is practice. Practice. You and I have discussed this many times. One day you reach true selflessness, that's all. You are."—he said, humbly. That moment Enrique's smile irradiated something indescribable that made it feel unreal.

I knew I was in the presence of greatness. There was an awesome luminescence, a mixture between love and truth, that permeated the whole room. It reached my bones: the Buddha.

"I'm impressed, what can I tell you?"— I asked, not expecting an answer—I began to perceive how august his presence was — "You reached …"

"I'm happy. And a carpenter. I see things with total clarity. Full stop."—An incredible feeling of happiness floated around him and reached me almost by osmosis.

"Are you doing anything else?" — I asked, a bit lost for words.

"If you love yourself, you love people, and there's not much more you can do…"

EAST MEETS WEST *

"Just as the farmer irrigates a field,
a fletcher fashions an arrow,
and a carpenter shapes a piece of wood,
so the sage tames his self."
- Dhammapada

I hope you enjoyed the first story in this book. The way I see it, short stories should include ideas the author wants to share with the reader. Often, these are ideas the author *must* somehow share. Maybe you are interested in getting to know a bit more about the subject. Not Enrique, not the story.

Unless you are the Dalai Lama, you cannot explain how to reach enlightenment. And also one wonders if enlightenment is actually possible. Here I discuss Buddha and Eastern philosophy in general. And the West, of course.

After the embrace, and the farewell, after the laughter in the garden, close to the driveway, that feeling of unreality did not go away.

"Where you goin'?" —asked the taxi driver without much enthusiasm.

"Holiday Inn. The one near the airport."

"OK. No problem."

I told him I noticed a bit of Russian in his accent. He said he came from Azerbaijan. He was going back to Baku in two weeks. His family had done very well with the oil boom. He was the only one—he said—who had missed the boat because he tried too hard. He had gone to America to become rich.

The idea in the first short story appears basic, but as far as I know it hasn't been explored by many people before. As you would have gathered by now, it is the possibility of somebody we know becoming really enlightened. Of a friend or an acquaintance being an incarnation of the Buddha. Unlikely. But possible.

Why is it unlikely? Well, very few people are known to have been enlightened. There are people who are knowledgeable, people who are wise, people who are wiser than the rest, but enlightened? Very few. Especially in the West. But we'll come back to this.

The idea is almost biographical, because my friend Enrique (not his real name) is an actual person. I only imagined the possibility of him attaining his dream. Moreover, it's about the status of Buddha. But not of Gautama, not an anecdote about Buddha himself, as you have seen.

Magicians never tell how they perform their tricks. That would kill the illusion. But a story-teller is not a magician. We are allowed to tell how we got an idea. How the idea became the story. And, as I express at the beginning, there are ideas one feels one has an obligation to share. There are messages that need to be passed, like batons, to our contemporaries and to future generations. One of these messages, the way I see it, is the fact that very influential people, people who have established benchmarks, people we admire, are also human; the fact that these people shared in our humanity, that they were part of a continuum of consciousness in time-space—like we are. Showing that a person we know very well may acquire the same qualities as one of them, that they may become one of them, proves that shared humanity.

Some years ago I painted a hand of Christ, nailed to the cross, but with enough detail for you to see his dirty fingernails. There was no blasphemy intended. I only wanted to point out that Jesus was as human as we are. In the Greek version of the Bible he was described as a *tekton*, a builder. I believe we can admire him even more if we feel that he shared in our humanity. That he had a body and a mind, just like ours. He had weaknesses. Whether you believe that he was God or not, that is a different story. It would be hard not to admit, however, that he was the most extraordinary man to have walked on this Earth.

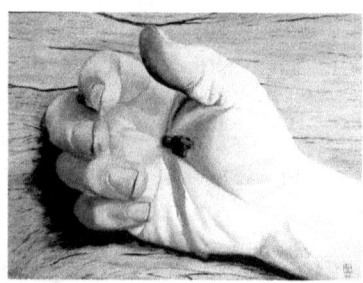

Incidentally, the hand that purports to be Christ's is actually Enrique's, who's a carpenter in real life. But let's talk about other people. What is it that makes some human beings so special? Why was Leonardo great? Was Winston Churchill a genius? Was Napoleon a genius? All of them were deeply flawed in one way or another. At the same time, very few people would dispute their greatness. I believe Buddha was indeed, a great man. And the concept he introduced, enlightenment, an inspiration.

I guess we can all agree that literature should be entertainment. I believe good literature should go beyond entertainment. Always. Maybe I am being too obvious here, but I'm not sure it is quite clear to all. Let me give you examples: what I'm talking about is the difference between bestsellers you read on the beach and Dostoyevsky. It's the difference between *The Da Vinci Code* and *Nineteen-eighty-four*. One is pure entertainment and the other one is entertainment with a message. The difference for the reader goes far beyond quality: one is opium and the other one is culture. Incidentally, I'm not claiming here that this particular story is good literature. According to the logic I have applied, all good literature needs a message. That doesn't mean that all literature with a message is good.

Going back to the original thoughts expressed here, why is the West not the best place to become enlightened? Well, there are important differences between East and West. The philosophical grounds on which the cultures are based are diametrically opposed. How is that? One is based on the self and the other one, on selflessness.

The West has been profoundly influenced by Christianity, which is a mixture of Judaism and Greek thought. In a way, the West is the product of Christianity. The individualism built into our culture comes from European languages and from Aristotelian philosophy but also from St Paul, St Augustine and St Thomas Aquinas, who added Greek thought to Jesus' message. This gave Aristotelian philosophy an aura of mysticism and Christianity an aura of truth. The "self" is central to both. Greek philosophy developed the idea of the individual soul and Christianity established the individual soul as an immortal one. In a way, the West grew together with Christianity. That growth included the appearance of concepts like objective truth and critical thinking. Science developed naturally out of those two. Objective truth is one of the logical conclusions of Western solipsism. According to it we are separate beings. Our ego is separate from the universe, therefore we can study the universe as an object. It is an object to be analysed. Hence, science. The East, and some currents of Greek thought, like Heraclitus, find that impossible, as the subject and the object are one and the same, and everything is dynamic, everything changes.

In the East, during the fifth to the fourth centuries BC, Siddharta Gautama founded a new movement later called Buddhism. Some consider it a religion; some, a philosophy; some, just a way of life. As we were saying, Buddha thought of life as something dynamic. Life passes. Time passes. Everything is transitory. Wanting to cling to something transitory as something permanent causes unhappiness. In short, he taught the way to let go of impermanent things and situations. Pretty much like Jesus, two centuries after his death he was declared the Saviour, the Buddha, the Enlightened One.

A legendary holy man called Bodhidharma took Buddhism from India to the South of China, where it grew. In the North, Confucianism was prevalent. It had common roots with Buddhism. They were both influenced by the teachings of a legendary character, Fu Xi, who had written his *I Ching*—or *Book of Changes*— a book and a divination system. It dates from the tenth century BC and includes principles and directives for a happy life. It has been described as "a living stream of deep human wisdom". Lao Tzu and Confucius were both familiar with the *I Ching*. Among other things, the I Ching teaches about modesty, peace and restraint. It also shows the negative influences of the ego: fear, anxiety, anger, desire, and other bad feelings.

From the South of China, Mahayana Buddhism went to Japan, where it derived into a similar type of Buddhism called Zazen, shortened to Zen. To this day, Zen coexists with Shinto, or ancestor worship.

The first contacts with the East, those of travellers like Marco Polo for instance, were few and far between. Europe was extremely interested in commerce with the East but also in their art, religions and philosophies. There was a physical obstacle between Europe and the far East: Islam.

Here, perhaps we should include some historical context. From the beginning of the eighth century, the Iberian Peninsula was invaded and occupied by the Moors. Europe was surrounded by warlike Muslim nations who made access to trade and contact with the Far East extremely difficult. Barbary Coast pirates and Ottomans roamed the Mediterranean, terrorising European coastal populations. The Crusades attempted to break through but eventually failed. In 1453 the Ottoman Turks took Constantinople, the last bastion of what had been the main Christian Empire left: Byzantium. By 1492, after the fall of the Muslim Kingdom of Granada to the Catholic Monarchs, Europe started its expansion to gain access to trade, particularly to spices, which were vital to keep foodstuffs edible for longer periods. The Portuguese and the Spanish commenced their expeditions towards what they called "the Indies" around Africa and across the Atlantic respectively. The Ottomans kept on advancing deep into Europe until in 1571, the Holy League, a coalition of Catholic states, inflicted a massive naval defeat on them at Lepanto. The Mediterranean was back in European hands. In the meantime, Portuguese and Spanish caravels had reached India, China and Japan. That was the beginning of a European fascination with their culture, philosophies and religions.

By the seventeenth and eighteenth centuries, Europeans had adopted decorative styles called *'chinoiserie'*, which copied Chinese motifs and techniques in furniture and materials.

But in Japan, after Jesuit missionaries achieved their first conversions to Christianity in the 16th century, the Tokugawa Shogunate, afraid of Western influence, closed the country for more than two hundred years (to understand this period, I recommend *'Silence'*, a movie by Martin Scorsese). In 1852-54 the Americans, under Admiral Perry, imposed the opening of trade which resulted in the Meiji Restoration. The West, again, became fascinated by the East and its aesthetics. *'Japanned'* lacquerwork imitated the sophisticated work of Japanese craftsmen and Giacomo Puccini composed *'Madama Butterfly'*.

The reopening of contact meant that people like Ernest Fenollosa, an American academic, could devote his life to the study of Japanese art, culture and literature. Fenollosa lived some time in Japan and eventually converted to Buddhism. He, and his assistant, Okakura Kakuzo, were highly influential in a revival of Japanese culture and a renewed academic interest in Buddhism in the West. During the time of his studies, Fenollosa discovered some ancient Chinese scrolls. Travelling monks had taken those rolls with the teachings of Buddha from China to Japan. Many of his discoveries were important. On Fenollosa's death, his widow donated his writings to Ezra Pound, who published translations of Chinese poetry and Noh theatre plays. In the meantime, authors like Herman Hesse (*Siddharta, The glass bead game*) and some time later Alan W Watts (*'The way of Zen', 'The Book'*) explained principles and practices to Western readers, or hinted about them in stories and novels.

During the fifties and sixties, Beat Generation writers Jack Kerouac and Allen Ginsberg, among others, began exploring Eastern ways and customs and experimenting with drugs. The American counterculture in particular based itself on Eastern philosophy and beliefs.

D T Suzuki, a Japanese academic and translator, who taught in several Western and Japanese universities, did a lot to popularise Eastern culture in the West with his book *'An introduction to Zen Buddhism'*.

From experimentations with meditation and Eastern art, literary vanguard artists, encouraged by academics like Timothy Leary, went directly to mushrooms, LSD, peyote and other psychedelic drugs. An offshoot of that was Carlos Castañeda's *'The teachings of Don Juan'*, followed by a series of books on shamanism that were mainly fictional.

The hippie movement took over from the Beatniks. George Harrison, later followed by the rest of *The Beatles*, befriended several Asian musicians—Ravi Shankar being the main star among them—which gave an incredible boost to the incursion into Eastern culture.

Following the musical and philosophical trend established by celebrities, many young people travelled to the East, especially India and Japan, looking for alternative ways in schools, *ashrams* and Zen monasteries. There were real *gurus, saddhus* and *swamis*, and bogus ones. Jiddu Krishnamurti was a real philosopher and author who wrote several books and had a huge following in the West. Others, like Bhagwan Shree Rajneesh (aka Osho), created cults that gathered thousands of adepts, with promises of alternative enlightenment that proved baseless.

A young Steve Jobs did his pilgrimage to India to find enlightenment. His devotion to Eastern thought and Zen Buddhism continued throughout his life. As the polymath and a business genius who found the connection between technology, design and the humanities, he probably gained some pleasure, maybe happiness, and shared some of that happiness among Apple devotees. But—I would venture—as an autistic man, enlightenment escaped him. According to Walter Isaacson, his biographer, he remained a Westerner at heart.

Apart from the contacts between East and West, the differences in their philosophies have kept both cultures as separate entities with few points in common.

Surprisingly, quantum mechanics has reached a point where science tends to agree with Buddhism. In the seventies, a book by Frijof Capra, a physicist ('The Tao of Physics') discussed exactly that.

Nowadays, more and more scientists agree that quantum mechanics does not seem to work together well with the concept of an objective reality (on which Western philosophy and science are based). There is one interpretation of quantum mechanics, however, that meshes seamlessly with Buddhist philosophy.

In the West there is, then, a renewed acceptance of the principles of Buddhism. Buddhism, in any case, doesn't need to prove a thing. It just is.

WILSON

*J*ovita was from Rocha. Uruguayan, like Miss Estela. She was so beautiful, Miss Estela, and so kind! Keeping the place clean, doing a bit of ironing and cooking for her was a breeze. All week, except Sundays. Jovita had her own bedroom. And she could keep Wilson with her. Wilson was born in Buenos Aires. He had just turned four.

Jovita answered the phone.

"Yes, Sir. Miss Estela is about to come back home. Yes, from Montevideo, yes, on the steamship. Whenever is convenient, Sir. Yes, I'll tell her. Thank you. Until then."

Georgie turned up one and a half hours later, agitated, wearing a beret. Estela opened the door. She had just arrived from Uruguay. He gave her the parcel wrapped up in manila paper. It contained a cardboard tube and a manuscript. Estela opened the parcel, gave the document a quick glance, and kissed him on the cheek. Just a peck, to say thank you. Few words were said. The moment remained like that, without closure, and a bit awkward. He left, as nervous as he had arrived.

Neither Miss Estela nor his mum were watching him. The little boy got closer to the Chinese lacquer table, his nose almost touching it, as if sniffing. He looked at the tube and the papers with his huge black eyes. He knew the man in the beret had left them there. Very slowly he stretched his hand until it touched the edge and then, again, pulled the tube and made it slide slowly towards his side of the table. The humidity took some time to evaporate from the bordeaux-colour lacquer. A trace of the little fingers remained—minuscule—on the glossy surface that looked more frozen than Chinese. Afterwards, in a hurry, he placed the tube waist-high, next to his shorts and examined it, secretly, even though he knew nobody was watching. He sat under the table and pointed the tube towards the window. There was not a lot of light, but what he saw was totally unreal.

"Woow!!"—he whispered, in amazement.

After looking through the tube and pointing it to all corners of the room, the boy got up and started hopping around the table. He had learnt to hop rhythmically the day before, so he thought it was something fantastic. The girl from the apartment across the hallway had taught him. The girl was also four years old but she was much more precocious, like all girls are.

Wilson was singing something that was a mixture between "María the princess... ate a schnitzel..." and "I am the queen of the seas". The lyrics were not altogether clear. The lyrics were also kind of girlish but, at four, he didn't care that much. The melody was a bit lost in the child's interpretation. The tube, hitting the table, provided all the rhythm.

What had to happen happened on the fifth turn around the table. The boy never quite found out if the tube had broken when it hit the table or if it had fallen off his hand.

The thing fell on the parquet floor with a clattering of broken glass. The boy looked at the brightness and the colours of the whole thing. There were bits of glass bouncing for a tenth of a second. They made the snapping noises that bits of glass make when they bounce on parquet flooring, until everything went silent once again. Something that looked like a large and very light iridescent marble rolled silently until it stopped under the grey French sofa next to the window.

The little boy rushed to the kitchen and grabbed his mama's skirt.

"What was that noise? What did you do, Wilson? Aw, this child is a real terror; he's going to kill me with all the troubles he gives me. One headache after the other... Wiiilsooon, loooook..." —Jovita walked towards the sitting room, wiping his hands with the apron and partially talking to a non-existent interlocutor, while the child was still grabbing her skirt, snivelling because he knew what was about to come.

Actually, all his suffering was limited to some scolding and a mild spanking on his bum. After that, Jovita went over the parquet flooring with the broom. What came then was all the crying and the tears, that were obviously exaggerated by fear, and all the acting, like saying: "I've learnt already, let's stop this". Then, the afternoon glass of milk and some time to play again. The floor was waxed and shiny. Wilson crawled around looking for something until he reached the edge of the French sofa.

Near the skirting board, under the sofa, a cold, strange, light shone eerily. The boy looked, curious. He never quite understood how that happened then, but he saw— simultaneously— everything in the world from all possible angles.

"Wow!!" —he said.

∾

THE STORY I have narrated took place in Buenos Aires, in the nineteen-forties. Argentine author Jorge Luis Borges had just written his most famous short story: *The Aleph*. In it he described a point that included all places in the world. He presented the manuscript to his then friend, Estela Canto— with whom he was hopelessly infatuated—together with a symbolic kaleidoscope. We know what happened to the kaleidoscope. Many years later, Estela sold the manuscript at Sotheby's for $27,760.-

In his book *Into the looking-glass Wood*, the author and later Director of the National Library of Argentina, Alberto Manguel, made reference to the episode in a very succinct and credible manner:

"In the summer of 1945 he told her that he wanted to write a story about a place that would be "all places in the world", and that he wanted to dedicate the story to her. Two or three days later he brought to her house a small package which, he said, contained the Aleph. Estela opened it. Inside was a small kaleidoscope which the

*maid's four-year-old son immediately broke." – MANGUEL, Alberto
- Into the looking-glass wood , Bloomsbury, London, 1999. –*

Some may doubt my version—improbable as it is—of the
events of that day, but I understand two things: the first one is
that when Borges said the parcel contained the Aleph he was
referring to the kaleidoscope and not the manuscript; the
second one is that he was so much in love with Estela Canto
that, literally, he would have given her the world. Also, and
most importantly, I have a first-hand witness of what
happened.

In Calle Libertad, almost reaching Five Corners, smack in the
middle of Recoleta, lives a retired psychology professor. Some
years ago he used to analyse the *tout-Buenos Aires*. These days
you can see him at Josephina's every Saturday morning,
having a latte. He always sits at the same table, always wears a
blue blazer and always reads La Prensa. He is my friend,
Wilson Ferreira.

BORGES AND THE BOOK OF SAND

*

*a*s you would have gathered by now, the purpose of these segments that follow the short stories is mainly to provide context. I believe the reader benefits from the extra details and can ponder the story in a more informed way.

The story you have just read, *Wilson*, is a real anecdote of the life of Jorge Luis Borges and also refers to *The Aleph*, but with a twist.

What can I say about Borges that is not in one of his biographies? Is there anything new anyone can add to the many anecdotes of his life and the many analyses of his writings? Well, we all know he never received the Nobel Prize for literature. We all know that Umberto Eco used his persona to create the murderous blind monk, Brother Jorge de Burgos, in *The name of the Rose*. We know his tomb is in Geneva, the city he loved the most after the city of his birth. Ahh, but I may have a new element to contribute about him.

This segment includes something that is never good: self-referencing. Inevitable in this case? I don't know. Perhaps a bit of an indulgence? Maybe. In any case, I have to be part of it.

To start, maybe I should say that, like so many other readers, I always felt a special affinity to the work of Borges. I admire his reasoning, so detached and cold, and his wide erudition. I admire how pure his Spanish is. I identify with many, many, of his ideas and also with his background. He came from an old Argentine family. I share the same love for Buenos Aires, for history, for Uruguay, for languages, and also for the United States. Shinto-like, he worshipped his father's ancestors, those "mysterious Portuguese" of the poem, and he revered the Acevedos on his mother's side. There was an undeniably Argentine quality to all he did. But, somehow, his writings and his ideas were largely universal.

I did not quite meet him; or maybe I did. It was a very superficial encounter. I will never know for certain. I spoke with him two or three minutes. This time, again, I have two witnesses, and an autograph to prove it.

∽

A BEAUTIFUL MORNING, radiant sun, and Buenos Aires, wearing her best finery. Florida was still Florida. I was taking a walk with my two teenage sons, after many years of Anglo-Saxon absence. I was showing them my Buenos Aires and, with paternal pride, allowing the city to get to know them. It was 1984 and we had come out of the Galerías Pacífico. We were slowly walking towards Plaza San Martín. When we reached the end of Florida, I almost automatically steered them towards Galería del Este. I remembered some water and perspex sculptures by Gyula Kosice I had seen a long time before, and a craft workshop called 'Los Picacobres'. Things had changed, but you could still smell the *confitería* and the aroma of coffee and croissants so typical of mornings in the city. The only recognisable thing now was the bookshop and maybe some *boutique* or other with Peruvian antiques and souvenirs. Sitting right there, in the bookshop, as he did every week—sporting an absent look—was Borges. Alone, with his walking stick.

I could not resist the temptation. I told the boys:

"Have a good look at that gentleman and try to remember what is about to happen."

I went straight to the counter and bought a copy of the *Complete Works*. After that I approached him with the boys and, book in hand, I asked him:

"Mr. Borges, would you do me the great honour of auto-graphing your book?"

"Of course"—he said with that slow and unmistakable voice of his.

He took a fountain pen out the inner pocket of his coat and, getting very, very close to the paper, he drew a tiny and shaky signature. Afterwards, feigning to look at me, he said:

"What I have just signed are the *Complete works*. But you have not read *The book of Sand*, have you?"

"I have read almost all of your work but I must confess I have not read *The book of Sand*."

"You have to read *The book of Sand*."

That moment I thought: "Yessss. C'mon, Borges, you're making a sale."

I thanked him and, without another word, I started to leave. The boys were a bit impatient then, but they still remember the moment. When I reached the door of the bookshop, he turned around in his chair, both hands on the walking stick, and insisted:

"Remember, *you* have to read *The book of Sand*."

Oftentimes one's interpretations of what the other person has said are just imagined or even false. A gesture, a word... The light at that particular moment. Something that feels unreal in an unexpected situation.

I guessed—I felt—a question mark in what he was telling me. For a while I thought it was more than a sale pitch. Why the insistence? Why the emphasis on the word *you*? Was he trying to tell me something? But everything was so perfect and I was so happy with my book and my autograph that I let it slip. We kept on walking, there were more anecdotes of my youth in Buenos Aires, we had lunch and eventually went back to Banfield.

With the years I read *The book of Sand* and re-read it, time and time again, as with all of his writings. The moments and the places I did that were totally different, totally unrelated: one month after I divorced; when I moved to Sydney; when I went back to Canberra; during some holidays in Bariloche; on a flight from San Francisco to Texas, and some other times I don't quite recall. The reality is, the stories in *The book of Sand* are not my favourite stories. But the book has something that makes it especially mine: Borges recommended this one to me.

There is nothing rational in this, but every time I read *The book of Sand*, in a mixture of superstition and rite, I look for the message, the hidden meaning. I have discovered rare coincidences. In *There are more things*, for instance, Borges mentions two places: Austin, Texas, one of my favourite cities and one I visit every time I go to the US, and Temperley, the suburb where I spent my childhood. That is rare. In other stories he does not mention Temperley (or Banfield). He always goes back to Adrogué, his favourite town in the South of Buenos Aires. Of course, that should not surprise anybody. There is no message, just coincidence.

But there may have been messages in other instances. My training as a linguist provided what is perhaps a different path: many times languages reveal secrets through errors. At one point Borges translates *'Esse est percipi'* and the translation, *'To be is to be portrayed,* is incorrect. Borges would have been incapable of such a mistake. This had to be on purpose. The sentence should have been *'To be is to be perceived'.*

My hobby, my obsession, is painting portraits. And I started painting them years after that meeting with him. Was Borges telling me that? Illogically and superstitiously I kept on looking for encrypted meanings coming through time-space.

But there were many other coincidences. In *Ulrica*, for instance, the main characters are a Norwegian woman and a Colombian man. One day, after reading it, I was thinking that those countries were so dissimilar that they would really have very few things in common. That same day, there was a piece of news about a new kind of waterpolo, an underwater version, and that the countries with the most enthusiasts were Norway and Colombia. Jung would have said "Synchronicity".

Borges, as usual, kept on talking through his erudition and his depth. Now I read all of his writings, not only *The book of Sand*, and find prophesies. Was Borges a prophet? Am I deranged in my old age? They are both possibilities.

A couple of years ago my two elder sons had an argument. They both wanted one of my self-portraits and the book signed by Borges. The matter was easily solved. The self-portrait went to Melbourne.

Until recently, there was a light green, thick, autographed book in my library. Now that book is in Sydney, in my eldest son's library. I am convinced that Borges talks to him as well. [1]

A CONSPIRACY AGAINST TIME

*M*iguel walked slowly, keeping his eyes on the little bike. Why had he called him Camilo? Well, he knew and that was enough. Nobody else needed to know. It had been an homage of his youth to two revolutionaries who had died before their time: Desmoulins and Cienfuegos. Both sacrificed by the revolutions they had started. Naming him after his heroes was like an echo of footsteps he admired; the boy was the symbol of his second chance. Or third chance, maybe. He had no doubt, however, that Camilo already was his own person.

Miguel watched Camilo pedalling ahead of him. He was not a toddler any more. Still, the moment filled him with true love for the boy. He had grown so much in five years! The crisp Canberra morning smelled of moss. Camilo's bicycle was leaving its imprint on the moist, yellowy leaves.

The walk to the University was long and full of mental potholes, like *"black holes in the sky"*... Pink Floyd—he thought —... fuck— he added a second or two later. It should have reminded him of Stephen Hawking. The thought stopped then and there. He had never fitted in academia, though.

He thought "Pink Floyd". Fuck, again...

Coprolaly and *coprofagia*, similar scientific terms but two very different meanings: swearing or eating shit". Always walking on the wrong side of normal.

Without rhyme or reason he recalled the strangest—and at the same time the most real—adventure of his life.

To GET to the Union Bar you had to climb up the staircase, which had walls covered in ads of people wanting accommodation, wanting to sell last year's books, or the odd guitar, (Ibanez or even other brands). As usual, at that time of day, the union was chock-a-block full of students. Also, as usual at that time, the place reeked of beer.

Werner—the chubby, long-haired angel—was waiting at the bar with the ever-present schooner in his hand. You could forgive him for polluting the conversation with terms like "viral structures" and "covalencies". A strange biologist, he also read other things. Sitting next to him, in a threadbare white skivvy, poor Donaldson was a deadringer for Garfunkel. Instead of mathematics, though, he taught nineteenth-century sociology. He was interested in the Industrial Revolution.

"Come, sit here, Miguel. So, what's up?... Hey, this one's my shout." (Up close, Werner's little eyes smiled in a nerdish kind of way).

Come on, man, you drinking with us, or you going to the other side of the billiard table 'cause that's where the girls are, you arsehole? —*¿Dónde vas, boludo?*" said Donaldson/Garfunkel in Spanish, with a very broad self-mocking Buenos Aires accent.

At that time, Miguel was thinking of comparisons between art and life. Literature and life. Life is stranger, he thought, although he knew the thought was commonplace.

"Shut up, Bruce, you sound nothing like a *porteño*. You exaggerate, dude" —complained Miguel, enjoying the beer more through his lips and nose than through his taste buds.

"What are we doing on the weekend? This place is so fucking boring we could be living in a postcard"—muttered Donaldson under his breath.

"I was waiting for Miguel to come to uhmm... to show you something *súper interesante*"—said Werner, also in his version of Spanish.

"Not again! Fatso is going to come up with an adventure like that time when he invited us to go out at night to puncture car tyres. Shit, man. Grow up."

"Hold on, hold on: maybe Werner has picked up the little redhead from the tutorial"—said Miguel, who trusted his friend.

∽

THEY WALKED, chatting and kicking stones, through the beautiful clumps of trees of the campus, three kids coming back from school. Crossing the little bridge on Sullivan's Creek, they dodged a group of bicycles and reached the building. That was the place where Werner did the things scientists do. The sign on the door read "Research School of Biological Sciences".

Once inside, they didn't stop at Werner's office. They stopped three doors down. Looking a bit like a Teutonic Balzac, he took a bunch of keys out of his pocket. The thick air in the room smelled of critters and mildew. The furniture had been modern in 1965. It was university issue and they all knew it had never looked too refined. The tables were of square metal tubing, black in colour, with formica tops. The two little armchairs, also black metal, upholstered in old shit-coloured sixties material. On top of the bookshelves—with more folders and papers than books—there were little cages with rats, one next to the other. Apart from that, the mess was inescapable, including heaps of papers and two fairly greasy computers.

"Nothing's formal here, everything's functional"— thought Donaldson tautologically, while he looked around, curious. Miguel's attention was caught by the little white labels. Very neat writing, in blue marker pen—he thought. They were all over the place, as though they were trying to deny in their own little way the huge mess that surrounded them. Miguel thought:—"This is so predictable, like everything Werner does"—he didn't know how wrong he was.

Officially, Werner was working on a project that, in the long run, would attempt to prove the existence of the fabled cytoskeleton. The Holy Grail of all biologists. He believed, passionately, that cells had an external structure. That external structure allowed them to function even after processes like ultra-fast spinning. Miguel and Donaldson already knew the subject by heart. Whenever they told Werner that the whole cytoskeleton thing was pure dogma, Werner would change the subject. They hoped the news had nothing to do with that.

On the larger table, in the middle of the room, there was a cage with a rat. In front of it, a McDonalds paper cup. The rat looked interested in something that was not them. Kind of curious. It walked fast from one side to the other, ignoring the visitors. Next to it, there was a plastic tray with another rat, dead and mummified dry.

"*Voilá*", said Werner, trying to sound multilingual. He also glowed with pride. That pride grew upwards from his neck, to his jaw, and ended in the smile of his eyes.

"*Voilá* what? Hey, mate, explain yourself. We're human beings, not biochemists like the other nerds you work with ." — Miguel was curious.

"OK, let me explain it to you. I don't have to tell you about Ian Wilmut and Dolly the lamb from the beginning, do I? The clone, you know. That rat is exactly the same, produced using almost the same methods. A rat clone. With the only difference that I made it all by myself."

"That's impressive, man. On the other hand, if other people have already done it, why repeat the thing?"—Donaldson was fascinated by the possibility, but couldn't help knocking it.

"You have to admit that the big guy here is a genius. Fuck, you should be Australian, Bruce, not a Yank. Cutting the tall poppies down is a local pastime, man. If you think…"

"But that's not all, gentlemen"—interrupted Werner, theatrically—"let me tell you a little story: around 1850, in Sydney Barracks, on Macquarie Street, there was a rat infestation. Rats would eat all the foodstuff the soldiers had and would steal their things. The fact is that in the end they called the pest controller, or something, and poisoned all the rats without mercy. Nowadays, in that very same place, there is a museum with an exhibition of all the things rats would steal. And also they have some dead rats from that period. Well, to make a long story short, that dead rat that you see there is one of those barrack rats from those days. And the live rat is a clone of the dead rat, not of a live one. Right now I'm about to produce a pig, which is almost finished. Anyway, this is my humble response to Spielberg and Wilmut, you guys. But this is real."—And here Werner changed his tone of voice, to a less jocular one—"You are the first ones to know."

"What are you going to do with it?" —asked Donaldson, already imagining *The boys from Brazil*.

"Gentlemen, we have the technology"— said Werner, mocking the guy from countless reruns of the *Six million dollar man*, and affecting control. He enjoyed the feeling of power that came with the experiment. Other than that, he didn't have the foggiest.

"Mate, you have created a monster. Mary Shelley would be proud of you"—Miguel was as nervous as Donaldson, but tried hard not to show it. He continued, joking—"When you finish with the piggy, you should try a gentleman. The sky's the limit."

"Too easy." —said Werner—mocking some accent from somewhere, as he usually did. He sounded a bit frivolous about the whole thing. Kind of scary.

"You crazy diamond"— thought Miguel— "Pink Floyd, again. Doesn't matter." He started humming *Che gelida manina*, very softly and purposely.

They chatted and joked, and downed a bottle of champers in plastic cups. Werner had taken the bottle out of a bar fridge, full of samples of something reddish brown in colour.

If allowed to grow from there without giving it a bit of thought, the matter could have serious ramifications, so they had to let it settle for a while. Of course, Werner was in charge. Some time later, the big guy confirmed that he had produced a healthy porker.

~

MIGUEL HAD ACHIEVED a marriage that was as comfortable as the wing chair where his father read the paper until he fell asleep every night. Tracey was relatively young, nice and Anglo. Generally, she was of the non-aggressive sort, although sometimes—out of nowhere—she would become a rabid feminist. Her latest essay, *"Latin references to Lars Porsenna in Arician tombs"* was nothing new, but it added evidence of the Etruscan occupation of Rome and had been a huge success in the Classics Department. Life was tranquil and *bourgeoise*. The couple had neither ambitions nor lust. Canberra was the ideal city for them. Without children, Miguel's house was a paradise of order and books, punctually paid with a mortgage and a monotony that weren't at all painful.

The phone rang. Miguel was correcting stacks of exams on the dining room table. A *prosciutto* and cheese roll—prepared following strict instructions from a Spaniard who had a little bar in Avenida de Mayo, in Buenos Aires—was part of the ceremony. The roll was not exactly what Argentinians call French bread, nor the cold meat the same as the one in the Argentine version. However, between the *prosciutto* from Yass and the Canberra bread, which were poor substitutes, the thing was quite edible, as Auntie Ernestina would have said.

"To be an Argentinian is to be in exile"—he said to himself. Commonplace, again. Food was the only real element of the mirage he had created about his birthplace. There was no Argentina. The thing was an iridescent and platonic reflection of something that existed out there in black and white. A pedestrian reality, indeed. His childhood was no more.

"Hello? Yes, Bruce. Yeah. Of course I have some ideas of my own. Listen. Why don't you come over and we talk about it? See you."— Two weeks had lapsed, but Donaldson was as excited as the evening they had seen Werner's rat.

Ten minutes later Bruce walked in. He was in a hurry. Didn't say a word. He sat on the sofa, next to the window. Miguel made himself comfortable in a Chinese chair in front of the sofa, and focussed his vision right behind Donaldson's prominent curls, on the bamboo that lived beyond the window pane. The colour green of the bamboo made him think of his mother, who loved the elegance of the leaves, and of Lin Yutang, who had asked for a bamboo to be planted in front of the window of his study. Coming back to the moment, he looked into his friend's face. There was no doubt that Garfunkel was there, but in the shadows and movement of his friend's face there was also the ghost of Harpo—Reality is so elusive because associations of ideas have multiple times and spaces, or time-spaces. That bamboo will always be mum/Lin Yutang; Donaldson will always be Garfunkel/Harpo—he thought to himself. A bit of nonsense he had baptised "quantum philosophy". Silly, but adding the word "quantum" to every new idea was fashionable those days.

"OK, what do we do now?"— said Miguel, opening the dialogue.

"Look, I think we've been both thinking about the same thing. So far nobody has talked about the possibility of bringing back some famous personality. Imagine Leonardo, Newton, Hieronymus Bosch, Picasso. I don't know... I have a short list. What do you think?" — Donaldson's voice trembled with anxiety.

"Yeah, I've been thinking about that too. Shit, what a responsibility! Don't you think? We should discuss ethical, moral and logistic problems, and acknowledge the limitations of the system, because the system has limitations. For instance, we would need to be absolutely certain that the remains are of that person. Let me tell you something: you can forget about Leonardo right now. You know that he died in Amboise a little bit before the fuckup with the Huguenots. It seems that when the thing blew up, the mob destroyed the cemetery and, by the time they realised there was a problem, the corpses were all over the place. To put together Leonardo's tomb they had to gather bits and pieces from the ground, anyway... a disaster, dude. Also, we should consider somebody this side of the Renaissance, don't you think? I don't know what sort of problems the big guy may have with very old human remains"— said Miguel, holding the telephone in one hand, about to call Werner

"Hello, is Dr Steinbrink there, please? Werner, is that you? Why don't you come over to my place if you have a minute? We're here with ma' main man Donaldson, talking about little sheep and piggies, if you know what I mean. Come on, mate, leave whatever you're doing and come over".

"He says he's coming."

"Imagine! It'll be like escaping time"—said Donaldson, excited. He had always been interested in cryogenics, and now displayed a semi-infantile enthusiasm in the project without even imagining to what point he would be involved in it.

"Look, Bruce. This is very interesting, but we have to be realistic. Anyway, listen… let's wait for Werner."

They chatted about all kinds of things. The conversation hovered, a bit artificially, around Kosovo and the Albanians. From there it went to pyramid selling, to the Wall Street Stock Exchange and then, capriciously, to the Bauhaus. When Werner arrived, about twenty minutes later, Miguel and Donaldson were still at it, discussing the theoretical and practical changes design had suffered during the nineteenth and twentieth centuries.

"Can you understand to what degree a group of original individuals like those is a historical rarity? Of course they're not like the Arts and Crafts movement, for instance, or these postmodernist fuckwits we have now. These dudes were something else. They were a bit obsessed with an exaggerated formalism, until Le Corbusier appeared on the scene."

"You, Argentinians"—interrupted Donaldson—"it's not culture. You people cannot stop the name-dropping. If you were so sophisticated your country wouldn't be where it is. You're a country of pretend-intellectuals. It's a socioeconomic phenomenon. Lack of originality, man."

"Come in, Werner, and wait a second. This guy doesn't understand."

"It's a way of communicating, person to person. Listen: Eco is a name dropper. Eco enjoys his monologues and loves to show off. Borges communicates. To communicate, in the etymological sense of the verb, is to look for points in common, points of reference. That's what you do when you meet somebody new and you ask them where they work, where they live and that. That's what Aboriginal Australians do in the same situation. Let me explain it to you. This is a dialogue between two aborigines who have just met:

"Do you know Mary Warrlpungi?"

"No".

"... what about Joe Nyulu?"

"No".

"... and Betty Ngurraar?"

"Yeah, she's my cousin"

" Ahhh, that girl is my granddaughter. So, you're my grandson too. You have to give me a cigarette."

"Do you understand? Click. That's where the communication lies. I know who you are and you know who I am. We may be showoffs, but when we discuss something seriously, we want to make sure the other person understands us. We want to make sure we're talking the same language. We look for the shared experience, can't you see? When I name a name, I expect you to know who that person is. Otherwise you should tell me you don't know them. But I digress..."

"OK, is this what you made me come here for?"—asked Werner, who was already getting bored with a conversation he did not understand all that much, nor was he interested in.

"What would you think of a clone of some very special personality? Bringing a genius back to the world?"

"But of course, I'd be happy to... wouldn't think it twice." — Werner appeared to be deciding then and there, but had thoroughly thought about it.

"OK, fine."— answered Miguel in a hurry, like closing a deal.

"Now, we would have to choose the person, and think how we're going to go about it, because it could cost a pretty penny"—said Donaldson, who was scared, but excited.

"Bruce suggested a few, Newton among them, and he also has a list I haven't seen. I would have liked Leonardo, but it's not possible. Uncertainty with the DNA and things"—Miguel was being cryptic.

"Both of them would've been good, but there's always the problem of how we're going to get the raw material. In the case of the rat, I had a friend who works in the museum and she gave me the specimen, no problem at all. With human beings, I don't know what you propose, because I refuse to go around digging up cemeteries. I think I have a solution you're both going to like. The guy was pure genius. Mainly militarily, and with some detractors, but also a statesman, legislator, etc" —said Werner.

"I'm not that convinced about the military bit, but he covers a few nice areas"— said Miguel, who originally had thought of Van Gogh, or somebody like that.

"OK, read my lips: Napoleon. He would be ideal. Let me tell you: in my office I have a clipping from an article that was in the Canberra Times couple of weeks ago, where I read that Bob Geldoff bought Napoleon's dick at an auction for an undisclosed sum. Yeah, it's grotesque but... it gave me the idea that, with an innocent little theft, we could get the raw material we need. Of course, I don't need a lot to get the DNA, so we don't need to ruin the poor guy's investment. What do you think?"—Werner gloated over his choice.

Miguel admired Napoleon, not because of the military glories or for the Code that bore his name: he admired the tenacity of the man that had been defeated but not vanquished, who fought after Elba with the whole world against him; he admired how he had imposed the *Ile de France* dialect as the official language and—more than anything else—he loved the relationship with Maria Walewska, such a delightful character. Donaldson was not totally convinced at the beginning, but eventually went along with it. The matter had been decided unanimously.

There was a long discussion on the repercussions of the project. All three knew what they were doing and assumed responsibility. There could be some negative consequences. In general, though, the risk was minimal and fairly remote.

"To start with, we have to understand that there is a great difference between resurrecting somebody and creating a clone,"—explained Werner—"Napoleon is dead. All his story and his circumstances are dead. Finished. This new person will have the same genetic features, but is not going to be the same person. 'Equal' does not mean 'identical'. You, Miguel, understand better than most the subtle semantic difference. He may be taller than Napoleon, although he wasn't actually short, since he's going to have a different diet. He may prefer different things and have different psychological complexes. In principle, the personality will be the same, but we don't know up to what point the environment—human and historical—will create different reactions to those he would have had. Fascinating! This is totally uncharted territory."

"Whatever we decide, right now, this very moment, anybody can make a clone of anybody else. We have no copyright on our genes. Weird, isn't it?" —Donaldson realised the immensity of the situation.

"And listen to this other one," —Miguel enjoyed the most twisted of possibilities—: "if I create a clone of myself and I bring him up, and that clone creates another clone, even if my number one version is not totally identical to my number three version. I could be my own grandfather. And so on and so on; that's an abomination not even the guys who wrote the Bible could have imagined, mate."

"I can assure you one thing"—added Werner, who kept on guaranteeing the adventure with his professional integrity— : "we will not bring an old virus, like the Spanish flu of 1918, or things like that. I make sure they're deactivated."

"Fuck, hadn't thought of that. That would be pretty ghastly"— Miguel was looking through the front window.

Tracey's red Corolla pulled up at the driveway. The conversation automatically went to the proposed cuts of the Liberal government to the academic budget.

"Hi, honey"—he said, kissing his wife.

∾

"*ALEA JACTA EST*" — thought Miguel.

Donaldson had just told him that he had spoken to his friend Felicity in London and that everything was ready.

"I hope we don't end up in gaol because of the first—illegal— part of the project."

Felicity had already liaised with Geldoff's housekeeper. After two weeks, the plan was beginning to take shape. Miguel and Werner were preparing their respective contributions. Donaldson had to get hold of the 'raw material'. The idea was that Felicity, having offered to pay one thousand pounds to the housekeeper for some pictures of the thing, would introduce Donaldson as a photographer working for *National Geographic*. Donaldson would travel to London looking very professional, camera and everything. Apart from that, he already had Werner's instructions as to how to obtain what they needed.

There were some very active days—a bit of a hassle—because Miguel and Donaldson were up to their ears in work, preparing programs for the following year. Werner had no problem because he had people who worked for him and who organised most of his teaching program. Two weeks later, Werner had everything in place for a major operation. Donaldson, after getting the Head of School to approve his program, left for London, with the camera hanging from his shoulder.

MIGUEL WAS LISTENING to a violin sonata by Rossini (something out of this world) when he got the email from Donaldson that everything had gone according to plan. What followed was a triangular maelstrom. It started when Donaldson—with great pomp—gave Werner a little brown parcel, wrapped in polythene, at a cafeteria in Sydney airport. After that, the whole thing centred on Werner's ability to extract the DNA from the sample. Werner, of course, didn't disappoint them. A little while after that, they got together at the Research School of Biological Sciences. All three of them were very circumspect because they understood that the step they were about to take was at once historical and inevitable.

"Look, Miguel" —said Werner— "here it is: ready as it ever will be. Bruce and I have done our bit. Now it's your part. I hope you do what you have to do."

That moment Werner sounded and looked kind of ceremonious, something that didn't quite suit his nerd image. Miguel now thought of him as a fat Germanic Merlin. —"Walt Disney" He associated the whole scene with Mickey Mouse, dressed as a magician, dancing with the mop. "Fuck, not even at a time like this"— Donaldson looked anxious. He had an infantile look that went well with the moment.

"Not the slightest problem, gentlemen, I can assure you"— Miguel, knew full well that it wasn't going to be easy.

∿

MIGUEL AND TRACEY'S love life started picking up after that time. The first occasion was Tracey's promotion to Associate Professor. They had gone back home after a beautiful dinner at the restaurant on Black Mountain Tower. A really delightful evening. One could do anything. The temperature was ideal. Tracey put a very old version of *Garota de Ipanema* on the HomePod. A Brazilian voice, pure satin, caressed them while Miguel prepared something to drink. The Martini glasses looked totally retro.

"Anything the matter, darling?"—asked Tracey, noticing a certain first-date nervousness that Miguel had not had for a long time.

"Of course not, hon. I was a bit peeved with Bruce today, that's all. I'll tell you tomorrow, not now. Here comes the man with the Martinis. Shaken, not stirred, as we all know."

After two drinks, Tracey felt extremely drowsy. That wasn't strange, considering the amount of phenobarbital Miguel had laced the drink with. Later, he picked her up and put her in bed very gently. It took a few minutes, although it didn't work that time. Apart from complaining that she felt a bit funny the following day, Tracey didn't suspect a thing. It took some persistence and two more romantic evenings. The night of the third attempt, Miguel fell asleep in Tracey's arms, dreaming of a swarm of bees in a field full of flowers.

~

THE YEARS HAD PASSED SO QUICKLY. It was unreal. Werner had already been given his full professorship at MIT and had gained fame with the cytoskeleton. Poor Donaldson had gone back to the States after the brain tumour was discovered. He had become President of the Cryogenic Association of America, a position he held until the end. Werner, faithful friend, had spent the last moments with him. In any case, Miguel knew the secret wasn't going anywhere.

~

CAMILO'S little bike stopped on the lawn, in front of the Library.

"Daddy, is the University yours?" —Camilo took off his helmet looking at the Menzies Library building.

"Of course not, darling. I only work here, like many other people, including your mum."— Miguel smiled condescendingly.

"This will all be yours. If I cannot buy it, I'll get it for you some other way. For you." —It was the promise of a five-year old, but you could tell he really meant it.

Miguel sat on his heels to give him a hug. The sun projected the library's shadow onto the lawns. At that point he noticed, for the first time, that determination, that shine of black steel in Camilo's eyes. [1]

CLONING *

$\mathcal{W}$hen I wrote 'A conspiracy…', the idea of cloning human beings felt much more remote than now.

No doubt the general idea of the story has dated. Also, I have added some minor amendments in this version that make it somewhat anachronistic (there were no HomePods in the 1990s, for instance; the ANU Union Bar in the story still is as it was in the those days and the Research School of Biological Sciences is now the Research School of Biology). I hope the validity of the story still holds though.

Before the fictional deed is done, at one point, one of the characters mentions the unlawfulness of what is about to happen. In actual fact, stealing raw material for cloning—that is, DNA —from cemeteries or anywhere else is a crime, and the mere idea of cloning humans poses countless questions, legal, bioethical and religious, among others.

I remember towards the end of the twentieth century, though, that everyone was very impressed by the creation of Dolly the sheep, and the possibilities that it opened up in terms of cloning.

What was accomplished that last decade of the twentieth century in the field of cloning was something amazing. And there have been many developments since then.

In 1996, Dr Ian Wilmut and his team at the Animal Breeding Research Station of the Roslin Institute succeeded in producing a pair of lambs from embryonic cells. Nothing like that had been achieved before. For that, Dr Wilmut received the Order of the British Empire. In 2002 he was also made Fellow of the Royal College of Surgeons.

The technicalities of the cloning of Dolly were imagined or copied to a certain extent in the story. Wilmut and his team removed the nucleus of an egg with the genetic material they needed. The ovum was fused then to the mammary cell of an adult individual. The egg commenced growing with the genetic material of the adult sheep. The team then implanted the embryo into a surrogate mother.

In the story, the first stages of the process are not explained (basically because, apart from Werner, nobody knows how the whole thing works). After that, Miguel implants the embryo. Again, that may not be possible without knowledge of the recipient. Please excuse my supine ignorance. The possibility of Tracey receiving the embryo without knowing—apart from being criminal and sexist—was too tempting not to be included.

We have seen that, irresponsible as they are, the characters in the story go beyond animal cloning and into human cloning.

This is a decision three academics make without a lot of careful analysis and consideration. It is unethical to say the least. The result is funny/ strange, but it could have been tragic. Again, we don't know what the future holds for Camilo. Obviously, what they did opens up possibilities that could be as horrendous as the Frankenstein monster. But then, what was unthinkable in 1996 is already happening. Mixed human, chimpanzee and gorilla embryos already exist.

The question is: is it possible to clone long-dead animal or human individuals? There have been talks of a group of Harvard academics trying to revive the woolly mammoth; and, in February this year, scientists cloned a black-footed ferret that was duplicated from a speciment that had died over thirty years ago. The main problem scientists have encountered so far with the mammoth is obtaining enough DNA which, apparently, is very difficult as nobody has found an intact and viable mammoth cell. In summary, it is possible, but extremely complicated.

That raises the question of the possibility of cloning any hominin, Denisovan, Homo Floriensis or Neanderthal individual. Sequencing the Neanderthal genome has already been done. Synthetically, it woud mean introducing Neanderthal chunks into a human stem cell. If that operation is repeated many times, theoretically it would be possible to clone a Neanderthal. So far, Denisovans and Floriensis remains have been much harder to find.

With the Neanderthals, leaving aside any ethical questions, the scientific problems are many, including the way Neanderthal mythochondria would react to being inserted into human stem cells. Their facial and pain-perception genes have already been inserted into mice and frogs. We can only imagine what could happen to a cloned Neanderthal individual in our society.

We now know that there is 1 to 4% of Neanderthal DNA in the bodies of people with European or Asian ancestry, as they interbred with humans and are the closest relative we have among historical primates.

Now scientists are concentrating on nerve and brain cells and the production of mini brains.

The study aims at determining how Neanderthal genes influenced brain development.

But the story goes beyond the cloning of humans for the sake of it. It proposes the possibility of cloning very special figures from history. As I mentioned before, that would raise countless legal, bioethical and religious issues. I read now on the web that many have been and are being proposed, among them Newton, Jefferson, Tesla, George Washington, etc.

The choice of Napoleon as the figure to be cloned was very simple. He was a genius with many incredible qualities; he had long-term plans for Europe, where he implemented many liberal reforms. First and foremost he was a statesman, a planner and a legislator. He also happened to be a very successful military leader, pretty much like Winston Churchill was in the twentieth century. Of course, he had defeats, like most warriors, but he never gave up. Nobody really knows the causes of his death in St Helena.

Napoleon's main contribution to history is the Napoleonic Code, on which the legal systems of many countries in the world are based. But he also abolished feudalism in Europe; promoted meritocracy, property rights, secular education and religious tolerance, among other principles that underpin democratic governments in the Western world.

Science and technology have given us many opportunities that were unthought of a few decades ago. Bringing back historical figures may be a conspiracy against time as the story suggests. It is also possible now and perhaps already happening somewhere.

THE ANT FARM

"[Gautama] also
possessed the awareness
that people cannot be neatly
divided into saints and sinners."
-Stephen Batchelor

*N*ormally for an interpreter/translator, listening to intercepted telephone calls or conversations from a device is just like any other job. There are some differences, though. In my case, it gave me ideas.

In general, from the word go, there's this thing that becomes immediately clear: there are two people speaking on the other side. You are on this side, listening in. There is this invisible barrier that is more than physical. Hard to explain. You are listening on this side and they cannot see you. They cannot hear you. They don't know you're there. But it's not as if you're spying on them. I think of it as an ant farm. They are constantly going around, frantically moving from one end to the other of this place, totally transparent to you. You watch them and study them. Maybe a lab assistant feels like that, watching microbes moving through the microscope. I don't know. Sometimes, it's like watching a movie. Some other times it's just sad. You feel sorry for them. They are also human beings. Thing is, if you're listening to them, it is because they are already doomed and they don't know it.

If you transcribe Arabic phone calls, your cases are probably terrorism-related. If you do Dari or Pashto, it could be terrorism or heroin. In my case, as a Spanish interpreter, I mainly deal with one crime: cocaine trafficking. The accents and the slangs I hear are mostly Colombian or Venezuelan, but also Bolivian, Mexican or Cuban. It doesn't matter. To an Argentinian, the accents sound colourful, sometimes funny, never quite real.

～

UNDER NORMAL CIRCUMSTANCES, the sticker on the flash drive would read *Lipstick-C* and it would have some numbers in red marker.

But now I was listening live. Deborah's panting sounded like a red flag. Imminent danger. Her voice was high-pitched and jittery. She needed urgent action. What was happening was very, very serious. I listened and transcribed:

"Fuck, Raúl, hurry up. I tell you I need the stuff straight away. This bastard says he's not leaving until I come out, and he's knocking on the door with a bat."

"*Haven't got a penny, kid. Do you get it? If I could, I would take ... OK, listen: let's do this. I catch a taxi and you pay me when I get to your place. How many papers do you need?*"

"*I don't know, bring four or five. Hurry up. I need you here in less than fifteen. As soon as you get here I pay you.*"

"*Sure, too easy.*"

"*But hurry up, man. 3:20 in the morning and this arsehole screaming here. The neighbours have already complained. What's worse, I'm scared he might get even noisier and somebody might call the cops.*"

"*Don't worry. I'll get dressed while I wait for the taxi. You go downstairs and talk to him behind the door see if you can calm him a bit until I get there.*"

"*OK, see you then*"—Deborah's sounded cool as usual again.

"*Ciao.*"

I took the headphones off, stretched a bit in the chair, and finally decided to call my Cuban handler. We'd been working together on this operation for a few months—in drug importation cases you often work with bilingual police officers. I knew what I had heard just then wasn't that important, but I called him to cover myself.

"Hello...¿howya doin', *chico?*" —I love feigning the Cuban accent.

"Hello. Man, stop fucking around this time of night, you idiot!... Roberto, what's wrong, brother? *¿Qué pasa?*"

"I've been listening to *Lipstick*. Deborah has problems with a client. She promised stuff and hasn't got any left. There is this guy who wants to break down the door. Raúl is going with some stuff, but if the guy keeps on making so much noise I'm scared the boys from Ashfield station may turn up and that would be the last thing we need."

"They have their orders, man. They know they can't touch these people. Don't worry. Let me sleep, bro. Tomorrow's going to be heavy for me."

"Sorry. I thought that maybe..."—Of course the call was warranted. Better be covered.

Anyway, that was the end of it for that night. Going back home, Oxford Street drag queens were having a ball, showing their best finery. There were groups and couples. Sydney's gay community was getting ready for *Mardi Gras* and life was a beautiful dress rehearsal. One of them, in a brightly-coloured tutu and a Qantas cap waved at me from a corner. Their celebrations were meant to be in-your-face. He waved one hand and threw the head and one leg backwards like in a fashion shoot.

"Jesus!"—I dispaired, tired— "it's so late and they have so much energy."

Driving home at dawn could be fresh and agreeable sometimes, but afterwards you had to go to sleep quickly. The day ended up a bit tight on one side and stretched on the other. Working nights was something the body didn't accept that easily.

"It's not bad, anyway"—I thought with a mixture of resignation and enthusiasm.— "In any case, I like the job."

I wondered when the cops would decide to stop the investigation. Maybe they would have to wait for some of them to come back from Colombia. There were two couples: Deborah, who was still dealing in Sydney and at the same time having an affair with Raúl. Nick, her Aussie husband, who was in Medellín with Laurita, Deborah's sister, and another guy, Matthew (actually Mateo) looking for a contact.

Perla, Raúl's wife—on a separate mission—had gone to Cali to talk to "the Lady". The Lady was a very dangerous character and she had to be careful. But Perla was from Cali and knew important people in the city.

The whole panorama sounds complicated until you get to listen to them and know their voices, their personalities and their quirks. Then you get to know them kind of intimately. You can hear them laughing, breathing, crying, begging, threatening, on the other side of the phone. In any case, that's why cops normally have charts on the wall, with all the photos with arrows, connections, names, places, etc.

IT WAS ABOUT two in the afternoon. I was really enjoying that cigarette. "After eating, sleeping and sex, there's nothing like a good cigarette"—I thought. The Homepod was playing *"Concierto de Aranjuez".* That guy could do anything he wanted with a guitar, so things couldn't be any better. Shame the *maté* was a bit cold, so I put the kettle on again. While pouring, I admitted to myself I had kept the *maté* habit because it was part of being Argentinian. *Maté* was nice, but it was a habit that could be easily dropped, especially in a place like Sydney, where you had to drive half an hour to buy one kilo of *Cruz de Malta*. And sometimes they didn't even have it: you had to buy Brazilian *yerba*, which was the worst. Brazilian music was nice and they played decent soccer, but they knew nothing about *maté*.

I had this idea to do with a drone. The idea kept on coming back. It was a good idea and, on top of that—I reasoned— I have a lot to offer. Now the idea was becoming even more interesting.

"Shit, this is hot"—I said aloud, pulling the silver straw that had got stuck to my lower lip.

It was painful—but the thought continued—it would be possible to get something to carry up to twenty kilos undetected. They can fly up to 250 kms which is a pretty good distance for a yacht. Some are meteorological, some for other scientific purposes. When the telephone rang I was thinking about talking to somebody I knew in the States. I checked the iPhone and—of course—it was Carla.

"Hello"— I barked out loud and a bit aggressive. I didn't like being interrupted, especially when I was working on this idea and it was becoming increasingly real.

"Hi, honey, you don't call me, you don't come to see me. You have totally forsaken me, Roberto. I have been leaving messages on your phone for a week, and nothing"—the complaint sounded warm and flattering.

"Darling, you know how these cases are" —that was lame, I thought— "I haven't gone out, I haven't had Saturdays or Sundays during the last three months. I come home, I sleep, I eat, and then back to work. You are the only person I see, apart from the Cuban and the girls from work. It's almost over. Couple of weeks, I reckon, at the most."

"What time do you start this evening?"

"Eight. Why don't you come over for a little while?"

"I'll come to pick you up and we can have a coffee in Paddington. That, if you promise me on the way back we stop at your place for a while, if you know what I mean."

"Sure, come over."

"Ciao. Love you."

~

THERE WAS this endless corridor between two rows of cubicles. The CID girls (CID meant Communication Intercept Department) looked as bored as usual in their headphones. They would paint their fingernails, watched videos on their iPads, or talk about guys. The whole scene was a picture Kafka could have painted. The Cuban was after one of them. I would often see him stopping at her cubicle to chat her up. It was funny.

That evening I had passed through all the security checks, had shown my ID twice and had swiped my card to open the door. That was the daily pilgrimage until I reached my cubicle.

The Cuban had one of those old-style moustaches. Rather than hiding the Colgate smile, it enhanced it. He was reading the transcription of the last flash drive. He was a good guy. In a suit and necktie he looked a bit out of character. The guy was colourful and Cuban even if he dressed like a monk. He had a *guayabera* shirt in his soul.

"How ya doin' brother?" —it was a friendly hello...

"Good, good, my friend. I see you've been reading the latest one. What do you think? I'm not sure about what you told me on the phone today."

"Well, before reading your transcript, I was listening to the *Makeup* line. I think Raúl doesn't know anything about it. Don't you think? I believe the guy is plain dumb. His wife hasn't told him anything. If you listen to all the *Makeup* conversations during September it would seem that the wife didn't tell him she was going to Cali to look for a contact. And Deborah hasn't said a word either. He sounds genuine. When he tells everybody that Perla went to Colombia to see her sick mother I believe he's fair dinkum. Anyway, that's the way I see it. That's my hunch."

"Yeah, yeah. You're right, he's a poor guy. Perla has conned him. He believes she's a saint. So, what happened today? How's the thing going on the other front?"

"It's looking good: they have been talking to a small guy and apparently they'll be getting twenty kilos... You'll hear the meeting in Medellín. Sound quality is not that good because it's from a device, not a phone. You'll work it out directly anyway, without looking at my transcript. At first they were a bit scared but now they sound very enthusiastic. As usual, some of these things may end up in problems but until now it appears they have been lucky. The Colombian police tell us they have transferred part of the money into the guy's account."

"What..., ah... so you have the details of all the accounts?"

"Yeah, man, our Colombian guys have everything."

"Listen... and nothing about the big boss?"

"No, the only thing we know about the boss, until now, is that he's in Melbourne."

"That guy is clever. It's like the Lady in Colombia. Nobody has seen her. And nobody has seen him either."

"No, that's right. The Colombian cops have a dossier on the Lady, but nobody can prove anything. And there are no recent photos either. "

"Perla seems to be doing OK, at least according to the last conversation I heard with a contact."

"It's all good. She knows everybody in Cali. I would say Perlita will get another five or ten kilos. They only problem they have is price. They cannot agree about it with the Lady; well, at least with the intermediary."

"And when are you guys going to start kicking doors in?"

"Hey, not yet. You've got to wait a little longer, *che*."

The Cuban wasn't very happy when I asked questions out of my area. Yes, we were good friends. Yes, both Latin American. But the Cuban belonged to that other club, a very exclusive one in these cases, and I didn't: he was the policeman. I was a civilian. There were questions you didn't ask and answers that were never forthcoming. As usual, that lack of trust kind of stopped the conversation. The Cuban excused himself. He couldn't come to have our usual coffee. He just started talking to another cop. I went back to doing my business. There was a bunch of flash drives from *Lipstick* and *Makeup*. I took a *Lipstick* one, as they were the more interesting ones, and plugged it into the laptop. The timer started running, and the clock marked the tenths of second, as usual.

~

I ASKED about the drone I had seen on the website. The guy was always smiling and had solutions and answers for everything. He smelled a bit of piss but, apart from that, he was an engineer and had detailed information. He wore a tweed jacket and rubber-soled shoes. He had an incredible number of small drones but also had contacts who had larger, more professional, ones. Apparently he was a founding member of one of the drone associations of Australia. I was very impressed. He knew a lot. While we were chatting, Carla made believe she was interested. She was looking at a desk-sized drone worth thousands. I could make friends without much problem, so I was making the guy feel important. But there was also the commercial target thing. I didn't look like the standard client, but you never knew. He bought the story that I had a company and was interested in commercial deliveries.

We ended up big friends. As I was leaving I promised I would translate a couple of blurbs and the guy was going to find out about how to use the weather forecast drone for deliveries, although he had already given me important info. I had a couple of names in the States and the name of the producers in Australia, basic details, price, models, and how to find more details on the web.

I took Carla to Chatswood for lunch, then we went back to Paddington and, while she was checking her mobile, I went to the computer to find out a bit more. I felt satisfied and at the same time, anxious.

∼

THE STICKER on the flash drive read *Lipstick*-C135. The timer, 24320. The clock, 02.40am. I started transcribing:

"Hello, it's you, my chubby love!" — Deborah's tone had changed from tough-street-smart to a mixture between dolly and mumsy—*"When are you coming back? Darling, I cannot wait to see you."*

"Hi baby. I'm so tired of being here, I want to be back home with you"—Nick adopted the same silly tone — *"How are you? What's the pup doing?"*

"I've got a cold, but more than anything I'm missing you a lot. She bit the sofa to shreds, so she can't come inside. The first day she howled so loud the neighbours complained. Anyway, she's always been a drama queen, but she's OK now. Other than chasing the birds like an idiot she's behaving. She's fast asleep now. How are you doing, honey?How's things?"

"All good. Very good. The hotel is nice. Things are dearer than I thought but everything's good. Laurita went out with Matt. I think our friends have organised a shipment and then we'll be able to go back home. The most important thing we've got to do is leaving everything organised the first time. All we know now is that we'll be sending ten books twice, you follow?"

"Yes, Nicky, yes. And everything comes addressed to the company?"

"Yeah. I didn't tell you. We had a bit of a problem because I got pissed off with our friends after the first delay. Things are different in South America and I realise that. I understand you have to be more patient. I'm OK now. And our friends have apologised."

"I'm glad. Apart from that, everything good?"

"Yeah, Perla called from Cali. I think the Lady wants to send ten more books, but there's nothing sure. Yeah, and we all have diarrhoea, including Laurita. So, it's very, very funny. People are right when they tell you not to drink the water."

"Good. Come back soon. And tell Laurita to call me, OK?"

"Of course, darling."

I finished the transcript, printed the document and put it on the stack with the other ones. That was the routine. I had to do transcriptions of all the drives they would leave, as much as possible, and put them on the in-box for the sargent to read them. That night I had five, and they were all *Makeup* ones.

I took a drive that read *Makeup*-C102 and plugged it into the machine. This was another mob. There were the usual beeps and sounds.

"Hi, Pedro, is that you?"—I knew Pedro but didn't recognise the other voice at all.

"Hi, how ya doin' little bro?"—I noted that Pedro treated the other one with extra familiarity. In a funny kind of way, in the underworld, that meant danger or respect.

"How's life, you poofter?"

"Here we are, and you, my man?"

"All good. What's happening with the family, the kids, the wife?"

"Good, brother. What can I do for you?"

"No, no, nothing. The Gentleman wants to know how things are going. He heard there was a problem with the system."

"Tell him it's all good. Tell him we're doing our thing, a small sample, together with the ones from Bogota, you know. Our friend already spoke with some of the people. We'll see."

"Good, my man, good."

"Tell me, Octavio, what are you doing?"

"All good, brother. Same old same old. Call me when you have any more news, will you?"

"Too easy. Ah, you motherfucker, I've got your old phones. Give me a land line, man ... Don't send it through WhatsApp. I've been having problems with that shit." —I smiled. I knew the cops had access to his WhatsApp account.

"How's that possible? Got a pen? Write it down, so...zero...three... nine...three....four..."— after hearing the Melbourne prefix, my heart started beating faster —*five...seven...six...seven...six... eight."*

"Six... eight..."— I could hear Raúl's echo. —*"repeat the fucking number to me, you lost me."*

"Zero-three-nine-three-four-five-seven-six-seven-six-eight. OK,bro, call me, OK?."

"Tell him so far no problem...OK. Ciao ciao."

The conversation was strange. People normally had three or four cell phones. No land lines at all—except for very important people—I imagined. Was there a connection with the boss? What was strange was passing the number over the phone. The prefix from Melbourne gave me the push I needed. I was very much aware I had something nobody else had. With a shaky hand, I wrote down "Octavio" and the number on a yellow Post-it paper. I folded it and put it in my pocket. Very carefully, I erased the last bit of conversation and put it back in the machine.

"..."

"Good, my man, good."

"Tell me, Octavio, what are you doing?"

"All good, brother. Same old same old. Call me when you have any more news, will you?"

"Too easy... (unintelligible)."

Those were the last words on the flash drive. I had erased the number. It was unintelligible. I did the transcription up to that point and put it on top of the stack with the other documents. I knew there was a master copy, but nobody would look at it, or compare this recording with the master. There was no reason to do it.

∾

NICK, Laurita and the other guy had returned from South America three days before. Perla had remained in Cali with her family and had called Raúl three times already: first, to say she was coming back on Monday; then, that her mother wanted her to stay a few days longer; and lastly that her flight had been cancelled and that there wasn't another one until the following week.

Life was beginning to get back to a routine that perhaps seemed normal to all of them. Nick and Deborah were visiting friends and getting ready for the arrival of the first batch. They had been eating out a lot, checking with Colombia every now and then, and watching TV. Laurita had gone to live with her boyfriend. I knew that wasn't going to last. Again, the feeling was the ant farm. The ants keep on moving without knowing what awaits them. I was very much aware that the big flood—cops kicking doors in—was coming and neither them nor I could do anything to prevent that abrupt end. I understood that and felt sorry for those poor lives because I had been watching them from such close range. —It's a bit like the Copenhagen syndrome—I would think. But there was something else. I needed to rebel against that law enforcement reality. The adventure was possible without the ant farm, I was sure. Admittedly, there were risks. Not being Colombian was a clear disadvantage.

The Cuban had been saying that in a few days there would be no more intercept of the *Lipstick* line. Did that mean the operation would be over? No answer.

As USUAL AT that time of morning, Pitt Street pedestrian mall was chock-a-block full of people. I left *Angus & Robertson* and went to Centre Point for a cuppa. First thing I noted on the iPad was a big *ABC* heading. I almost dropped it: after an operation that had lasted over one year, the Australian Federal Police and the Crime Authority had infiltrated and detained a number of members of a drug-trafficking syndicate. A cocaine shipment had been seized. It contained more than twenty-five kilos that were adhered to the inside of the plastic wrapping of magazines. There were names, photos and the history of the whole operation. Nick, Deborah and Laurita were already inside. Raúl, who apparently had nothing to do with the importation, had been interrogated. His house had been searched with a fine tooth comb. Perla had remained isolated in Cali. In any case—I thought—she was going to be brought back to face the music. Colombia was signatory to a mutual extradition treaty, so she had no hope in hell.

I HAD MADE up my mind. I wanted to show them my drone idea. But before that I had to call Carla.

"Honey…"—just through my tone of voice, Carla knew an excuse was coming up. I was leaving for a while, something she wasn't going to like— "…the case is over. Only thing is I will have to go away for a couple of weeks. The cops are sending me somewhere else. I can't tell you any more, you know, but I'll call you from wherever I am."

"What do you mean you can't tell me? You always told me we don't have secrets with each other."

"You know what these guys are like. They always have that spy mentality. And if you happen to tell anybody it could cost me. They wouldn't give me any more work, don't you know, honey? But don't worry. I'll call you. If I don't call you every day, at least every couple of days, OK?"

"No, it's not OK, but if you have to do it I will have to put up with it, don't you think?"

"Big kiss, honey."

"Bye, darling, kiss. Call me, OK?"

MY NEXT PHONE call was to the *Hilton on the Park* to make the booking. I had already booked the flight with Qantas, had the boarding pass on my iPhone wallet. It was for six am the following morning. That would give me enough time to do what I had to do. First thing, I had to go to the Crime Commission to tell them I wouldn't be available for a couple of weeks.

The Cuban was there, waiting. He was flashing a huge smile.

"So you caught them all, *chico?*

"What do you think, kid? They weren't expecting it. At all."

"What sentence will they get? What do you reckon?"

"Look, Roberto, I think at least twelve years, and that includes Nick, Deborah, Laurita and Perla, when we get her back here. Raúl, we don't know. Maybe he had nothing to do with it."

"Hey, shame about Laurita. Nice-looking girl that one, don't you think?"

"Well, nice-looking and everything, she'll be inside for a while."

"Tell me, what happened with the other one, Nick's friend?"

"Who, Matthew...? Mateo was one of our operatives. Didn't you know?"—the Cuban loved the whole situation; of course he knew nobody had told me—"...That's the interesting part in these jobs. Most of the times, apart from listening in, we know what they're doing from the inside, even if we miss something. We're always in control."

I smiled a bit, thinking that they didn't know everything all the time. The small chat went on for a while with the Cuban and the sergeant. I then told them I had a very urgent translation and wouldn't be available for a couple of weeks but, if they wanted, they could keep any extra flash drives for me to work with. There was no hurry now, until the hearing. *Makeup* was going to stay open for another week, I was told, but they would keep everything for me; in any case nothing they could say would be important any more.

~

I SLEPT THROUGH TAKE OFF, had my Coke and crackers, and what followed was an uneventful flight. When I woke up we were landing in Tullamarine. With only cabin luggage and my backpack, I eluded the carousel. I headed straight for the taxi rank. The rain was typical Melbourne and the taxi driver was Sikh, of course, turban and everything. He chatted, smiled and moved his head sideways, as expected. It had been smooth sailing so far.

I walked in the room, sat on the bed and got the yellow Post-it out of my pocket. Getting Octavio to call me back took several tries. I knew he was going to be suspicious at the beginning, and I also knew the whole move could be dangerous. I was determined, however, to take it to its final consequences. At first, hearing my own voice on the phone talking to Octavio sounded unreal. It was like having split into two and being able to watch myself at the beginning of a new, unreal, stage of my life.

I could be very convincing when I wanted to. That was the best weapon I had as an encyclopaedia salesman, long ago and far away, in a Buenos Aires that was becoming fuzzier and fuzzier every day. I knew very well the products I was selling: my knowledge of the CID and the idea of the drone. I explained everything to Octavio, especially the details to do with the drone, including some technical minutiae. It had a range of several hundred kms and carry twenty-five kgs per flight. The range was enough for any yacht outside Australia's territorial waters. It was possible to fine tune the flight with an iPhone more than two thousand metres away after takeoff and before landing. The second product was even more attractive: I had inside information of how the cops operated and what they knew. I was sure that would sound very attractive to anybody in the trade. In the end, I convinced Octavio. But that was only the beginning. The Gentleman had the final word and maybe he didn't want to see me. I wasn't Colombian.

~

THE WAITING room was classy without being ostentatious. I hadn't seen anything like that in Australia: the *boiserie*, the original Pissarro on the wall, the *Aubusson* rug and the Louis XV *bergères* were all for real. Nothing like the cheap gangster I had imagined. My thoughts and adrenaline were running at a thousand miles per hour. "Everything looks French—I thought—maybe the guy is not Colombian".

The door opened and a warm smile came out with a friendly, welcoming, hand. The Gentleman wore the gray hair on his temples with elegance. He had no affectations. A powerful man, he could be charming when he wanted.

The accent from Buenos Aires took me by surprise. In a strange kind of way I felt immediately at ease. It was like being home.

"Come in, Salinas. It's a pleasure to meet you. So you have a drone that would be ideal for us? I'm all ears. A cup of coffee? But tell me about you: whereabouts in Buenos Aires do you come from?"

THE REALITY OF THE JOB *

There are many perspectives to the story. The adventure, i.e., the character wants something totally new. He realises he has the possibility of an adventure and of a life different from what he has been doing so far. The technology: he has the idea of the drone and wants to implement it regardless of whether it is legal or ilegal. The perjury and the treason: he has sworn to abide by the confidentiality and privacy regulations of his employer. He breaches absolutely every rule and goes to work with the criminals and spy for them. He knows there is danger involved from both sides, but still does it. Rather than the money, the attraction appears to be the adrenaline rush. In the end he goes undercover but on the wrong side of undercover. He will infiltrate the police force. The only thing in his favour is that oftentimes you cannot tell a saint from a sinner.

The story ends with the surprise of finding that the "gentleman", the big boss, is an Argentinian. That is highly unlikely, as a very high percentage of the criminals involved in those activities are either Colombian or Mexican. There are other Latin Americans, of course, but they are rare.

Law enforcement agencies employ linguists all over the world. Many work for agencies, translating, interpreting, decoding encrypted messages or doing intelligence tasks. Most language work for law enforcement has to do with intercepts. They can be live or recorded. They can be from a telephone call or from a device. Those could be from a bug or from a recorder pointed to the speakers. As I explain in the story, surveillance is mostly to do with terrorism or drugs. In the case of Spanish it is definitely drugs. More specifically, cocaine.

Surveillance work is quite an experience. You are in a movie but it is real. As the character says at the beginning of the story, you listen and the criminals don't know you are there. Some of the people involved are in danger, you can feel it most of the time, especially when they are establishing the contacts, regardless of their references. Criminals suspect everybody, even their friends. All of the time. When there is undercover work involved, the danger is quite evident and imminent. Something very bad can happen any time. You can sense it. It is in the voice of the operatives.

In my experience, at least, what happens in the story is exactly the way it is in real life. The way soldiers describe war: a lot of waiting. Most of the time you hear small people chatting about things that are totally inconsequential. Until something happens.

You do not know who the big boss is. You rarely hear them. When you do it is brief and it is very clear that it is them.

The other thing about surveillance work is that it is engrossing, as probably most police work is. You get to know the characters fairly well. You know what to expect of them. You can guess their next move. Very often you feel sorry for them. And many times you get to see them in court, before the judge hands down their sentence. Then you hear "Twenty-one years" and you think "There goes a life".

BEYOND TIME

"Con te partirò
Su navi per mari
Che io lo so
No, no, non esistono più
Con te io li vivrò."
-Andrea Bocelli

*I*f you squinted, the rows of soldiers looked really real. You could imagine what the battle looked like from a hill. After a lot of research and reflection, I had decided on the colour for the Persian cavalry, spoke to Graham and agreed on next week. Graham had all the Greeks ready, so we could do the battle of Plataea without further ado.

Painting the boots of a Persian cavalry soldier, a bit lost in my thoughts, I was revisiting the way Mardonius had lost the unloseable battle. Mardonius had given Plataea to the Greeks actually on a platter. The Persians had to go back to Asia. Truth is poor Mardonius had been conned big time; great actors, those smart-arse Greeks.

"Pancho, you're at it again with the toy soldiers! It's a joke, you're almost forty-five, playing like kids with those other big morons! "—Julia's voice sounded tired rather than aggressive.

"Listen, I'm not going to ask you to understand, because I've already explained it to you a thousand times and it doesn't seem to be getting through. I repeat, however: these are not toy soldiers. These models only help us visualise the tactics and strategies of the generals." —I assured her, a bit frustrated.

After a short while the frustration actually took over, so I cleaned the paintbrushes and placed them neatly in the little wooden box with the enamels.

"Maybe she's right,"—I thought, almost agreeing—"this is the typical escape of my librarian friends. Perhaps emotionally I'm ten years old and I don't realise it. Anyway, nothing we can do about it."

My thoughts rumbled in the dark silence of the bedroom. It was slowly dawning and the bed was a huge sandwich of weariness and disappointment.

"That reflection coming through the slit in the blind is a pain. Fuck. I wonder if all of this is just a crisis? How are we going to end up? She's dreaming, poor thing— maybe if I give her a little shake. Julia grumbled a bit, whispered something unintelligible, and turned the other way, pulling with her arm most of the quilt. Softly but firmly, tug by little tug, the usurped quilt came back to me."

"The Malvinas" —I thought—" if Menéndez had had the balls, or maybe if they had raised the ante with all the planes from the beginning, in one go, as I thought. The whole hog... fuck."

The horizon was slowly turning red. A magpie warbled his early hello. My thoughts were going nowhere—*Fenêtre, finestra,* ¿why do we say *"ventana"* in Spanish? —I was totally awake by now— The Visigoths, with their Germanic things; window, windhole. This is definitely a critical period. I can feel a big change coming up. Of course, anything is going to be better than this depression in this bed, in a rented house. Five twenty-five in the morning. Insomnia is nothing but the inability to stop thinking.

"Croce, croce delizia..." (Verdi could express emotions in three words!) "Is it love? No, it's impossible. Probably closer to being weird. Maybe insane?"

But I did fall asleep. Profoundly. I dreamed about a prairie full of daffodils. From there, the dream strangely took me to a bachelor pad I shared with some friends in Calle Libertad. The whole place was half asleep in the grayish light of dawn. Julia was waiting for me in a huge bed. The bathroom was totally dark. At one point I was hanging my white shirt on the back of a chair when a voice came from the hallway, behind the door. It whispered my name. Fear paralysed me as it always does in dreams. I knew I could look through the spy hole but I stayed frozen.

～

I HAD PREPARED breakfast as I did every day without exception: cereal for me and honey on toast for Julia. Twinings *Irish Breakfast* for me and decaf coffee for Julia. It was funny but I could do it automatically. No thinking. That routine gave me a feeling of safety. I finished my last sip of tea and went outside.

In Canberra, winter mornings are a mixture of cold, magpies warbling and misty gardens. Neighbours' driveways and steam coming out of exhaust pipes.

"Hurry up, Julia, I'm late."— I yelled impatient, standing next to the car.

"Hey, what do you want? You spend an hour shaving and now you take it out on me."

She closed the door and kind of trotted into the car, knees together, holding the handbag under her arm. She smelled of perfume and kid glove. It was a morning smell that reminded me of Buenos Aires, although in Buenos Aires it would include the smell of the city in the morning, that is, coffee, toast and black tobacco.

"How ya doin' Greg? Doesn't feel like going to work, does it?" — I waved. The neighbour answered from the distance, smiling a reply nobody could hear or cared about.

What followed was, rather than a conversation, a car chat, a busy going-to-work car chat. King's Avenue trees frozen behind, their profiles beautifully cold and fuzzy, as the car accelerated. Julia crossed her legs.

"She's still hot for her age"—I thought/felt— *"Muda d'acento e di pensier...* still with Verdi. He was a genius, but kind of sexist, even for his times"—it took a while for me not to look at her legs. There was something in me, however, that was far away from all that.

"Thursday… payday."—said Julia, talking to herself— "Could you spare some time to buy the present for the kids' wedding, honey?" —Julia's voice stretched towards the end, in imploring mode.

"There are two things that really bother me: one, that you think I'm the errand boy, and two, buying presents. Why don't you take a minute to do that, since you have all the shops right next to your office?"

"Okaaay, temper, temper, hon; it's not a present for mum. Just drop me off here before the light goes green."

After leaving Civic, the car went on automatic pilot past Lake Burley Griffin, through the roundabout and the bridge, and got into the National Library's parking lot, like attracted by a huge magnet. The air coming from the lake was cold. I hurried up a bit. Henry Moore's sculpture, reclining Etruscan style, saw me passing but showed no particular interest in me. The Library/Parthenon welcomed me with a warm breeze that came from above and then grew to the size of the entrance hall. I said hello to all the smiling faces walking past, emphasising their names:

"Dave…"

"G'day, Pancho!"

"Marsha,… what's happening?"

"Hi, Pancho!"

"Ben…"

That was part of the ritual and I now followed it instinctively. Other than that, life in the Library had its own culture. I felt a bit repelled by the pompousness of some librarians, but I had learnt to live with them without showing it. Got to my desk, carefully put on the white gloves and pulled the first box of manuscripts of the day from the shelf. The label read "Trelawney Family– Correspondence 1850-1950 – Box 48".

I saw the handwriting and could not help feeling those butterflies in the stomach, again.

~

"St Patrick's 15th of April, 1862.

My dear Mary:

What's my brother-in-law doing?

Poor papá. He's such a beautiful person, and so proper. I am very excited with the ball at Duntroon. They have invited the gentleman I told you about, who has just returned from Sydney! Wouldn't that be wonderful? I am organising a new dress. It's gray but with a pearly shine. I want you to see it. I am keeping my fingers crossed. Anyway, it's in God's hands.

A big, big kiss for you and for my beautiful little niece, from your adoring sister.

Emily"

"I am near you again. We're spending time kind of together and you cannot even see me. I know, this is getting ridiculous. Don't you think? Nothing worse than falling in love (or becoming obsessed maybe?) at this moment in life. Especially when timing is so incredibly off. "

~

MEG'S CURLS were like a red lighthouse in the cafeteria. She wasn't particularly beautiful, especially when compared to some of the younger girls flapping their wings during morning tea or lunchtime. But—at forty—she could flash a sexy smile that would dazzle a librarian or two without much effort. I asked if it was OK to join her. She assented, so I sat down with her. We had met at the Translators' Association and had exchanged hellos and looked at each other some years ago. Then, her long hair was a flame, and she wore a kaftan and Indian sandals. Those were days when I still thought writing was just something *hip*, not something you had to do to avoid death.

"Yeah, so... I thought I had seen you around *Manuscripts*. So you spent a couple of years in South America? How does it feel, having to come back to this mausoleum?"—Meg's questions, fired machinegun-style, included no hint of irony or malice. The voice was a bit raspy, which is something I love in a woman.

"Look, South America is not all tango and Julio Iglesias, like you guys sometimes think. And having to come back to work here: well, I'm attracted to luxury; tell me, apart from the Ritz Carlton, where else do you get white marble toilets?"—I replied— "Also, as you know, salaries are among the best."

Meg's laughter floated noisy above the cafeteria's hushed conversations. We had a good time, chatting of times past and friends in common. By the time we realised we had to go back to work everybody else had disappeared.

Wendy was no teenager but, somehow, she had a smile full of metal braces and rubber bands. She was the Director of *Manu-*

scripts. Not only was she interested in what the people in her section were doing, but she made a big effort to show it. She came very close to me.

"Hi, Pancho,"—she leaned on one of the boxes—"how's this going? Isn't it great?"

"Wendy, what an honour to have you here"—I said, surprised —"all this correspondence is in such good shape, and the fact that the family kept it together for such a long time: nothing short of miraculous."

"Not only are the Trelawneys a very old family in this area, they're also related to a few very important people of their time. Very well-connected, even in Britain. They donated their collection to the Library, together with sabres, uniforms and other things, that ended up in the War Memorial. I understand the whole thing was valued at more than half a million. Not that money would mean a lot to them, they own ten thousand acres near Michelago and heaps of money in properties here in town. So, what do you think so far? "

"Look, I spent most of last week organising and cataloguing all of George's correspondence from World War I, when he was in Palestine with the Light Horse Brigade. It's difficult to explain up to what point you get to know somebody from the letters that person writes. You cannot imagine… when I opened the telegram informing the mother that George had been killed and how he had died I felt that mother's pain very deeply. I don't know; it ruined the rest of my day. I couldn't stop thinking about that poor woman. You get really involved. It's like watching a movie, but you know the characters are for real, they're people like us, with feelings. Now it's been a few days that I've been reading Emily's letters to her sister."

"Ah, yeah: Mary, the one who lived near Tuggeranong, married to the guy on the five-dollar note"—Wendy interrupted. Knowing the details was important to her.

"Yes, her, but there are also letters from Emily to other relatives and friends, you know, they begin in 1858 and go on for something like twenty-five years. Emily is so prolific and she writes in so much detail. Of course, back in the day they would write every day, sometimes twice a day, even at such a short distance, because there were no phones."

Wendy went back to her office, leaving in her wake a trail of Anaïs Anaïs, which bothered me a bit because it was Julia's perfume and it caused dangerously confusing feelings. The other thing about Wendy was braces at forty-something. Come on!—*Vanitas vanitatum*, I thought, but Emily's letters, even smelling of musty old paper, were all that interested me.

She must have been a beautiful human being. Generous to a fault, and amazingly feminine. All of that energy and activities, all that perspired through her correspondence was about making happy the people she loved. Emily never spoke ill of anybody, she was always giving great advice, was clever and had an incredible sense of humour. As I read her correspondence, even the bits that weren't that happy, there was a smile on my face. —Her writing transmitted an essence, all of her own, that passed from one letter to the next one. The essence impregnated my white gloves and stayed with me long after I left the Library.

I had been trying to fight that obsession. At that point I could not consider it something morbid, though. I knew I was prone to that kind of thing. I really needed to distract myself without thinking too much about it. However, more than once I would find myself going, alone, to visit St John's cemetery. The grayish marble, with the name Trelawney, in letters that had once been gilded, served as a special backdrop to feelings that I was not imagining, I was sure. They were as real as the white gloves I kept in my pocket.

I had seen her in a photo with all the family: a very blurry image. It had the diffused, daguerreotype effect that dead people acquire in pictures. You could barely see the oval of her face. She had very intense, very sad eyes. The black dress with a high collar reminded me of my grand aunts. She wore her hair a bit like the main character in the movie "The piano". I could even imagine her hands. I knew she played the piano and loved Chopin. Sometimes I could almost hear her, caressing *Prelude in D "Raindrop"* with her long fingers. My favourite.

~

"MY DEAREST MARY:

How is my beautiful baby today? And Helen? Ah, I wish I could spend more time with them. God will decide when.

Papá, as usual, extremely busy. The congregation keeps on growing.

Well, have to go. Sally McNamara wants me to help her with the dinner she is preparing. I believe she is rapidly losing her eyesight. She does not want people to find out, though.

An enormous kiss for my little angels and another one for you.

Your loving sister,

Emily"

I glanced at the watch. Two to five. Took off the white gloves and put the jacket on. I came out of the lift slowly and ceremoniously, said hello to everyone in the hall, librarian style. — In a hurry, but with a lot of dignity, what the fuck— I said to myself, thinking of my grandfather, who had been mayor of Curuzú Cuatiá.

∼

THE TOOLBOX with the soldiers was in the boot of the car. This time I was the Russians. It was at Graham's, who was in charge of the French. Graham had prepared a table with Austerlitz in incredible detail. Stephen Goodhope had the Austrians, so everyone was looking forward to it.

Truth is I would have wanted Gettysburg. What was fascinating was the fact that the Confederation didn't exist any more. The South had died but was still there. There was something fascinating about that. Like Biafra, like Acquitaine. Like so many other ideas/realities that had disappeared but were still physically there. Right then, maybe by coincidence, Andrea Bocelli was singing: *"in navi, su mari che, io lo so, no, no, non esistono più"*. Seas that don't exist any more. Wow.

I was kind of floating in the car, driving but not totally conscious, going towards Weetangera, again, automatically. Graham waited, placing his cuirassiers. I parked right next to his driveway when some girl—on the same playlist—was singing an amazing version of *Vivere*. I could not leave the car. Staying a bit longer meant I could enjoy the delight of her voice. She repeated *"vivere, cercando ancora il grande amore..."*. "To live, still waiting for that grand love". Sometimes, I'm sure, that grand love never comes. There must be something wrong with me, I thought. Where is all this romanticism coming from? I have always been a normal guy, maybe a bit on the spectrum. Except for the dreams, of course. Crying because of a song is something really stupid—I picked up the toolbox and, wiping my eyes, I walked to the door. I left behind the unreal reality of the car and the music.

"Hi, man. How ya doin' Graham? Ready for action?"—I had left my funny world and was getting into a real world of ideal soldiers without smell of gunpowder or horseshit on their boots. I got comfortable on the couch and, while I stretched my hand to take the cup of tea, the birds-eye view of Austerlitz was becoming something like a movie.

∼

FOR WEEKS JULIA had suspected I was having an affair. She knew things were not normal.

When I got home, I saw Julia's note on the kitchen table. She had gone to Kyrstie's to play backgammon. She was going to be late. I didn't need to wait for her.

There was nothing on the ABC News. I searched Netflix, AppleTV and YouTube. The search exasperated me. It also bored me to such an extent that my eyes slowly surrendered to the beige environment where dreams begin.

∼

THE DREAM WAS VIVID. And lucid. It was part of a recurrent series where I go to a town that is "my" town. The houses and shops are all red brick, with sculptures and reliefs and vaulted arcades coming out of them, also of red brick. The town is a reflection of all the towns and cities I've lived in. There is no logic to the place. There's a glass-covered bridge on one of the main streets. My aunt's mansion is also there, but only during the night. There is a street that winds down from a hill. That is where the Portuguese and the Vietnamese come from. The church is red inside and has black coffins high in the middle of the nave. I go to that church every now and then. It is not scary but I find it strange. Every single time.

This dream was more vivid than usual. I had gone to the country riding a special sulky. I couldn't see the horse, but it was there. That part of the country happened to be Michelago. It was also Braidwood.

There was this twilight in the house. As I walked around it I could see things a bit more clearly. I remembered that the ancient Hebrews separated night from day with a very simple method: the moment you can distinguish a black thread of cotton from a white one.

Emily happened to be in the hallway. She was crying.

"Emily? What are you doing here? Are you OK?"

"There is no present. I'm only in the past. I was. I am not."

"How do you know? You're here now. In this dream. Because it's a dream. And right now my town is Braidwood."

"Yes, I know. I remember my niece. And my sister. I cannot see papá, though. I saw you last time at St John's. And somehow I know you too... You read my letters. Last time I knocked on your door. I even called you. You didn't come because something else was happening. I think you were scared."

"You know what, Emily? I'm a little bit scared right now. Even in this dream."

"I know you watch me. You think I cannot feel it but I can. I like it, you know? It's flattering. And also, there are things in you that I like a lot. You're a librarian and you cried reading my letters."

"I know I'm dreaming, but… can this be real?"

"Yes."—she whispered, holding my hand.

I looked at my hand… and hers in mine. That's the way to know you're in charge in a lucid dream. I consciously walked, holding her hand. She followed me towards the door.

"I believe it's real too. Strange, but real. We both believe it's dreamy real."

"I will have to go soon"—Emily turned her face towards me, very close—"are you coming?" —the question was clear. She stared right into my eyes.

"Emily, let me think…"

"The only thing between us is time."

There was a kiss. A real kiss.

JULIA PULLED the keyring out of her handbag and opened the door. It was well into the morning. Pancho was barefoot, eyes wide open, looking at her with a big smile on his face. He was dead. There was total chaos and everything was out of character.

The big screen was on YouTube and there was a wide row of icons at the bottom. There was also a bottle of Coke half spilt on the carpet. The remote was next to him, with a Japanese bowl and a spoon.

There was no letter, no message, no explanation. A few days later, Julia went through the files in the computer: there was absolutely nothing.

The Canberra Times reported that Inspector J. Bennett, of the Australian Federal Police, had said there were no suspicious circumstances but that any further details would be included in the Coroner's findings. They would be issued the following week.

LOVE BEYOND TIME *

*T*he only purpose of the short story is just telling a tale. However, this particular story also raises several questions about love and also about death. One of the questions is whether it is possible to fall in love with, or to have a crush on, somebody you don't know personally.

Fans of famous musicians, actors, sports people or other celebrities appear to do so. So, it is possible for someone slightly unbalanced, not necessarily pathological, to "fall in love" like that. Some of them are totally obsessed with their particular celebrity. They are convinced that they are in love, but that does not actually happen in a real life situation. If you fall in love (not in an emotionally unbalanced or pathological way), it is usually with somebody you know personally. If you have a crush on somebody you see on a TV screen, for instance, you may fall in love with the stage persona, but you know nothing about the actual human being behind the mask.

So, not being directly personal, the involvement with the person is actually an idealised situation. That kind of love we can describe as platonic. Platonic love is a spiritual or emotional connection with the other, ideal, person. You think you know the person because of their actions, opinions or worldviews. It may or may not involve any sexual attraction. The moment there is sexual intimacy, lines and boundaries are blurred. There have been cases of actual liaisons between fans and celebrities.

The romantic love men felt for women in the West appears to have begun as a type of platonic love in the South of France, reaching Sicily, and then the whole of Italy and Spain. The idea of romantic love was not discussed before then. It developed during the eleventh century, the period of the troubadours. It all commenced as a literary tradition that emphasised nobility and chivalry. Women were idealised to the point where they were viewed as saintly.

By the thirteenth century Dante had helped courtly love migrate from Sicily to Tuscany, where he developed his *Dolce Stil Nuovo* (or *Sweet New Style*) on the basis of his love for Beatrice. She was loved and admired to the point where, at the end of his *Paradiso*, Dante placed her in Heaven, near God. Their love of course was never consummated.

Dante was emulated by a group of Florentine poets that became famous for their courtly songs and poems. So, Italian literary tradition commenced with Dante Alighieri, Guido Cavalcanti, Cino da Pistoia and other brilliant literary men.

Petrarch, following in their footsteps, invented the sonnet, and sung his love for beautiful Laura, again, a love that could never be consummated.

But I have digressed. We know it is possible, then, to develop some kind of romantic feeling for somebody you don't know or are barely acquainted with. Let's go back to the questions raised in the story.

Would it be possible to fall in love with somebody much younger or much older? There was a 1996 drama movie in Argentina, *Besos en la frente* (*Kisses on the forehead*), starring China Zorrilla and Leonardo Sbraglia, based on a true story, where an 80-year-old grand dame falls in love with a 26-year-old playwright. The story was written by Jacobo Langsner, who was the playwright in real life. And there are many cases of older men falling for much younger women. In that sense, age appears to be no barrier to falling in love.

Would it be possible to be in love with somebody who is dead? Often, widows and widowers love their dead spouses long after they have died. That appears to be a fairly common occurrence. The difference here is that they intimately knew the person who is now dead.

So, maybe we should rephrase the question: would it be possible to *fall* in love with somebody who is already dead? In the case of the story, Pancho, the protagonist, has read many letters written by the object of his affection. As in the case of the fans, who fall in love with the stage persona of their celebrities, the new question that comes up is: how much do you get to know a person by reading their correspondence? Even when that correspondence was not addressed to you and was written many decades or even a century before you read it?

Well, as somebody who has read many letters written by different people in different ages, I have my ideas. As you have probably gathered, the situation is similar to listening to telephonic intercepts. You are a witness to the way the person behaves in certain situations. You get the feeling that you know some individuals quite intimately, even if they are not even aware of your existence. It is literally being a fly on the wall. You probably get to like some people or end up disliking some others. In some cases, the one-sided connection with that person in particular may develop into a strong empathy towards the person. If the listener or the witness is not well balanced emotionally, or if they have some kind of psychiatric condition, it is quite possible that their sad situation could lead to hopeless depression. In the case of Pancho, it leads to his suicide.

The story requires no judgment on our part. It is what happens to a man who falls in love with a woman. In this case, she is dead.

COINCIDENCES

To Jorge,
who's part
of this story.

*O*ftentimes we talk about coincidences, but the term encompasses many types. Some of them are tiny, some are big, and some are colossal. This story is about colossal.

Tiny ones happen every day. Before I go into colossal I have two examples of big to give an idea of magnitude. A point of reference. For instance:

Early seventies. Like many young people in those days, a friend of mine did his *grand tour* of Europe, but he did it twentieth-century style: Jorge wore his backpack, travelled in trains, hitch-hiked, walked and biked through Europe with his Norwegian girlfriend. Somewhere near Oslo they met this American hippie from Philadelphia; let's call him Troy. A typical young American, Troy was chatty and extremely friendly. They decided to go from there to Paris together. In Paris they spent one day visiting the sights and then parted ways, wishing each other a happy life. Weeks later, Jorge and Ingrid were admiring some old church near Villarossa, smack in the centre of Sicily. There was Troy, again. After some laughter, coffees and a sandwich, they said goodbye once more. At that point, Troy told them he was going to Morocco, to visit a friend.

A month later, Jorge and Ingrid met Troy in Toulouse, near the ruins of an Albigensian castle. This time there was surprise and laughter, coffees and then the usual goodbyes.

To cut a long story short, during the next seven weeks, Jorge met Troy in Huelva (at the railway station, five o'clock in the morning); Fuendetodos, Aragón, in a bookshop, and coming out of a toilet, in a restaurant near Chinchón. That last time—Jorge told me—he heard Troy's scream and laughter before turning around and seeing him. To their young minds, reality seemed funny. It was also inexplicable.

Many people I know have stories like Jorge's. This one I heard first-hand, from the person who experienced it himself. How do you explain coincidences of that magnitude?

I HEARD about another amazing coincidence first-hand, from the person who experienced it: this young Australian woman on holidays with her husband in Denmark. They were staying at a boarding house and, one breakfast, they sat next to an old English lady at the dining room. The old lady was curious about their accent.

"Are you Australian? I have a friend in Australia." – she said.

"Yes, we are. Australia is a large country. Where does your friend live?"

"She lives in Canberra; she's an architect."

"Ah, we are from Canberra, and so am I. I'm a landscape architect."

"Yes, she's a landscape architect too. Actually, she's not a friend. She's my goddaughter, the daughter of a dear friend I haven't seen for ages. Her name is Monica Greaves."

Again, to cut a long story short, Monica was talking to her godmother. Amazing coincidence.

The way I see it, we're basically threads of consciousness that wander around, living through time-space, which we observe but often fail to understand.

I cannot explain coincidences, and there are some real-life examples that are quite amazing.

WHAT I'LL TELL you next are two war stories. Same war but a rather weird connection. A colossal coincidence. If you don't believe how things happened I cannot say I blame you.

The year was 1971. I was working as a library assistant at the Law Library of the Australian National University, in Canberra. Indexing law journals and magazines wasn't the best job in the world, nor was it the most interesting. It barely paid the bills. But, in my late twenties, married, with two children, it was reasonable. My only other choice was going back to labouring in the building industry. Not my thing, really.

Every working day, mid morning, the janitor would bring a stack of the law journals for me to work with. And we would chat, have a smoke and, very often, share morning coffee. We were just workmates but ended up developing something close to a friendship.

Ray Sommers was almost fifty (extremely old), balding, had an eye that pointed right—regardless of what the other eye was doing—, chain-smoked cheap cigarettes, and his fingers were stained by nicotine to an extent I had never seen before.

After quite a few coffee breaks and countless cigarettes, I learnt he had been a prisoner of war of the Japanese during World War II.

He was from Wagga Wagga, but for some reason had enlisted in Melbourne when he was barely eighteen. After a few weeks training, the whole 22nd Brigade, his brigade, had been assigned to Singapore. When the Japanese invaded, they resisted some weeks in Malaysia until, overwhelmed, had to retreat South, to Singapore. What happened next confused everybody. When the Japanese entered the city, General Percival surrendered without a fight. All the soldiers were taken prisoner and sent to work on the railway.

An enthusiast of anything Japanese, I was very interested in the experience.

"Ray, did you end up learning Japanese?"

"I probably could have, but I really hated the bastards. We were very hungry and they were cruel and extremely mean to us. You cannot imagine how cruel they were."

"For instance?"

"For instance they broke my fingers more than once. And they would need no excuse to beat the shit out of us."

"Ouch!"

"Yeah, they were mean arseholes."

After that, I didn't make any more comments about the Japanese. He told me many of their atrocities, which were really hard to believe.

Late in 1944, a group of them was taken to Japan, to work in some prison camp there. The ship that was carrying them was sunk by an American submarine, but he had survived and, having been rescued by the Japanese, was taken to a work camp called Sakata, in Japan.

One winter morning—very cold, as they usually are in Canberra— we were having our "smoko" and coffee outside, when he told me what he thought was the saddest thing that had happened to him. After Japan, he had gone home. His brother, Roger, two years older than him, had been killed on Anzio beach. Ray's father took him to the bedroom Ray and his brother had shared before the war and he noticed that Roger's personal effects were on his bed. Roger's beloved Rolleiflex was there too. Ray asked his dad whether he had developed the film in the camera. His dad hadn't thought about it. When Ray took the roll to be developed, the photos were no longer salvageable, so he didn't even have a memory of the last days of his brother. The thought depressed him for months.

Fast forward many years.

Late nineteen nineties. I'm in Austin, Texas. My third wife has an American father. We get along famously. While we are in Texas, on our annual visits, Jim and I chat, drink Manhattans and play gin rummy.

Jim was a lovely, tough old guy.

For many years he had worked as an oil engineer for Getty Oil Co.

Earlier on, when he was nineteen, during the war years, Jim Cardwell had gone from his native South Carolina to California to enlist in the Navy. He underwent the normal training and was assigned to the mighty Essex, the fastest aircraft carrier America had, and the first of twenty-two carriers in the Essex class.

Every game of gin rummy included anecdotes of his time in the Pacific. The carrier had been in several battles. Jim's job on board was to make sure the planes were in good shape before launch. He would carry out all pre-flight checks required and then report to the "shooter", the catapult officer, who would give the final OK. All the sailors on the flight deck were constantly alert about the kamikaze. And the attacks did happen.

When I asked him about them, he told me there were a couple of occasions they would come so close you could see the Japanese pilots' faces.

The kamikaze had actually hit the Essex once, he told me. It was after Leyte, in the Philippines. Late in November, they were on one of the decks below—I can't remember if he told me the third deck. They had been watching a Clark Gable movie. All of a sudden, sirens roared and they heard the "battle stations" cry. Everyone had scrambled to their positions. Jim remembered he had turned around as he was running upstairs and had seen the movie still on and most of the chairs in total chaos. He couldn't forget that moment.

As he was reaching the flight deck he heard the explosion. There were many injured and some casualties, some of Jim's flight deck mates included.

He told me something that had happened after the Japanese surrender.

They were spending time on R&R in occupied Japan. Groups of sailors, marines and soldiers caroused around certain areas of the waterfront in Tokyo. They were not free to go anywhere else and any contact with the Japanese had to be handled with care. He then added:

"I never visited Australia during the war, but I did meet some Australians in Tokyo. We had drinks with them. A few of them had been POWs who had been taken to Japan and were about to go home. I remember them clearly. I sat at a bar next to a guy from a place called Mugga Mugga or something. The poor guy had spent three and a half years as a prisoner in Burma. He was looking forward to going home even though his father had written to him that his brother had died during the Anzio landing, and..."

I never told him, but I knew the end of the story.

EVENTS WITHOUT EXPLANATION
*

*"Aristotle was by far a less able thinker than Plato
... he was completely overwhelmed by Plato".*
-Wolfgang Pauli

The observation of time and space has always occupied brilliant minds, has always been a magnet for them—perhaps we should talk about time-space, as Einstein dictated last century. And, of course, there are phenomena closely related to time-space, like chaos, luck, and probability. We have seen one example of big coincidence, or maybe repeated coincidence. Inexplicable encounters in time-space.

Stephen Hawking—almost esoterically—described three types of time (all of them more or less chaos-related) and talked about the shape of time. I'm not going to enter into the details, as you can imagine. Too complicated.

~

IN THIS SEGMENT I am not going to discuss coincidence so much as draw some conclusions from ideas that came to my mind many, many, years ago.

I was involved in another big coincidence this year: some friends of mine who love caravanning met somebody implicated in one of my police cases in a caravan park in Far North Queensland. I cannot discuss it in detail because the case is not totally closed.

Anyway, I'll try and make this segment brief.

Books have always been more than an important part of my life. They have been central to my life. It began when I was a young child.

My grandmother taught me how to read when I was four. At about age five, mum gave me a book by Constancio C Vigil, a famous children's author in Spanish in those days. The book was called 'Juan Pirincho'. It was a sad story about a little bird who was very sick. He didn't eat well, he was thin, his face looked like that of a monkey, and sometimes he seemed crazy. He wanted to get well and so he asked all of his friends and everyone else how to get better. They all came up with different cures for his sickness. The parrot said he had to eat bread soaked in milk or water. Other birds gave him their own ideas based on what they did themselves. The woodpecker said that he had to use his beak to peck into trees. Maybe he needed ants in his nest, maybe he had too many feathers in his tail. Nothing worked. Eventually he saw a bird doctor and the doctor cured him. My conclusion as a five-year old was that all of them were right but that truth was flexible. Juan Pirincho had found his own truth.

Later in life, when I was about eleven, I heard dad talk about the Unified Fields Theory, the basics of which he tried to explain, but it was all beyond my comprehension. All I understood then was that nobody knew the whole truth.

And much, much later, studying Italian at uni, I came across Luigi Pirandello, who was also obsessed with the scientific concept of objective truth. At that point I understood that objective truth was actually a very useful construct but that it didn't really exist. Of course, friends with scientific minds were not impressed with my ideas. And they are still not impressed.

Studying philosophy, I discovered that Heraclitus' ideas—which I have discussed elsewhere in this book—were not readily accepted in the West. They were not accepted because they clashed with Aristotelian philosophy. He talked about space and time and dynamics, about his famous river and how things changed. While critical thinking and science analysed and dissected, for Heraclitus everything flowed. There was a place for holistic thinking where, sometimes, things could be explained differently and dynamically. Somehow, there was a connection with buddhist thought, which I have also discussed in this book.

But the most amazing thing is that, whenever you read about science and how science cannot find all the answers in terms of truth and reality; whenever you read about objective truth and things like Schrödinger's cat—the one in the paradox—you end up discovering the strained relationship between quantum physics and the rest of science. The elusive Unified Fields. And then two names pop up: Niels Bohr and Wolfgang Pauli. Together with other scientists of the early 20th century they were among the first to study quantum physics.

Time passes. We all know that. We also move from one place to the other.

Leonardo Da Vinci noticed a similarity and used a beautiful visual metaphor to compare time and space: a moving point creates a line in space; a moving instant results in time.

Carl Jung, an analytical psychologist interested in Eastern philosophy, studied coincidence: a set of circumstances that are related but are not causally linked. In 1930 he came up with the term *"synchronicity"*. By 1952, after many years of interest in the subject, Jung published a book entitled *"Synchronicity: an acausal connecting Principle"*. The book contained a study by Wolfgang Pauli who, through his involvement in quantum physics and mechanics, was also interested in coincidence. The view of synchronicity from a mainstream scientific perspective is that it is indistinguishable from coincidence: its only explanation is chance, that is, an explanation based on statistics and probability.

Reading many definitions of coincidence by scientists and technologists I arrived at the conclusion that they really do not explain how coincidence occurs. Pretty much the same way that science cannot explain many occurrences in quantum mechanics.

Plato said that if science contradicts itself, a new theory must be developed. If we are to believe him, we need a new philosophical basis of science to explain quantum physics phenomena (and other phenomena, such as coincidence).

Heraclitus proposed that the way up is the same as the way down. Truths vary according to perspective. Juan Pirincho would have agreed.

THE METHOD TO PASS
BIOCHEMISTRY

"*I* know perfectly well what I'm talking about. I have direct experience in this. Were an encyclopaedic education be introduced in this country, Australia would be one of the cultural centres of the world. Do you follow?: ...of the world. The problem here is that innate Anglo thing about exaggerating anything to do with human rights. The system has to give you an option, even when you end up fucking up. Of course, kids choose all the easy subjects: Art and Photography are number one and two on the list. Problem is that then you have guys who go to uni and don't know that Burkina Faso is a country or that during Newton's time the United Kingdom was not a kingdom but a parliamentary commonwealth similar to a republic. In Argentina, like in many other Spanish-speaking countries, encyclopaedic education could be established because in those countries a certain general culture is a *sine qua non* for any occupation and because, you have to admit it, people are educated, what the heck. On the other hand, it was also easy because we don't give a shit about individual rights. But look, having said that, from personal experience I can tell you that the application of the system can be fairly flexible.

Let me tell you, in my case, that flexibility came combined with one of the most beautiful episodes you can imagine. Something that actually changed my life. It's a topic that may have other ethical and moral connotations but that, for me, was something more than beautiful. Maybe I was just lucky, maybe not.

I know it's not easy for you to understand, from the perspective of these, your times, and because you live here, in Australia, but look: to explain to you how these things can happen, you have to imagine you are seventeen, it's 1960 and you live in the Argentina I knew when I was your age.

At seventeen, there are times when there are girls and times of girl-drought. You're in the middle of a drought. On top of that, Marcela has just dumped you. You haven't dumped her. When it comes to girls, dumping or being dumped is incredibly important. If your self-esteem could be measured with a thermometer, you would be a few degrees below zero. Of course, those things are not shared. Not even with the best of friends. On the surface you are all smiles and you make believe you are so cool and popular. But, as your mum always says, still waters run deep.

Let's say that at school things don't look much better. Well, right now, the way you see it, life's a piece of shit:

1. Adrogué High is the centre of the known world.
2. You spend much of your life in the centre of the known world.
3. School is not going well, hence, life is shit.

(It appears to be a good philosophical principle. Or is it a mathematical principle? And if you're so good at these things, how come you don't pass mathematics?).

In high school the passing score is seven. Anything below seven and you have to sit a test in December. If it is below three you sit a test in March. If you fail in March you cannot proceed to the following year. In your case, you pass the easy ones, but fail or almost fail the important subjects. In Mathematics you have no possible salvation: you go directly to the March test. That means hell, without a chance to go to purgatory. (The problem with Mathematics is Dr Wiesenthal. That woman is Attila the Hun. And you are easily terrorised). Physics is a dicey one. Biochemistry is also dicey. Very dicey. Psychology: only if you get the same grade you got last term.

The weather is absolutely ideal. Springtime in Adrogué is almost as beautiful as Autumn. All you have to do is walk those blocks that take you from the railway station to the school. The walk from the railway station to the school is like a funnel: you always end up in the school. The warmer weather is almost here and school becomes an imposition. At this time of year the imposition is almost unbearable. You have been thinking about the party on Saturday. This is the season when the best parties are held. Boys normally wear a suit or white jacket and black trousers; girls wear very nice dresses, but they're never long or too formal. The norm is that balls begin with rock *Bill Haley and the Comets* type and end with boleros by *Los Panchos*, or with some other very slow, very romantic, music.

Your friend Jorge Rey is leaning on the window of the bookshop looking cool. Looking cool is looking like Jean-Paul

Belmondo. As you get closer you realise that Jorge holds the cigarette between his teeth.

"What are you doing, you idiot? Smoke properly, will you? Who do you think you are? — Your laughter is condescending. Jorge chooses to ignore you because he continues looking cool and is also watching Conti's little sister, who's getting better by the day."

"Kid, you're never going to learn."—Jorge lowers the sunglasses towards the tip of his nose and looks at you with the superiority of someone who's in the know. After that, he touches his lips with his thumb, waiting for Tina Conti to look at him. She continues walking, books resting on her hips, without turning her head for even the briefest second.

"*Cosa facciamo?* Do you want to go in?" —the question implies going anywhere else except to school.

"No. Today we should skip school. Why don't we go to the zoo? Look at that sky, man. Let's get out of here. Shall we?"

"Let's go."

The train. The coffee shop in Palermo. The walk to La Biela. The walk through Alvear. Girls everywhere. How can people live without having to go to school all these beautiful mornings? And you have to spend those mornings inside, bored out of your mind and having to stare at Dr Wiesenthal's bitter face. On top of that, when you play truant, when you can enjoy what the rest of the world enjoys, you get that guilty feeling that doesn't go until the following day.

~

TALKING ABOUT THE FOLLOWING DAY, you have Literature, although there's no problem with that one, because Toto Estrada is such a great guy. Estrada talks to students as human beings, not young morons. He has achieved something close to a miracle with this class. Because making Martínez like Spanish literature is like a miracle. Also, he has made us read a few books that were not on the program, and has awakened in you an interest in the Renaissance and the Reformation that, as he says, were critical times for European culture. You can say that Toto is the best. He doesn't mind getting off the subject and he can chat with Jorge and you as if you were his friends, or as if you were adults.

Another problem you have is Psychology: Dr Duval is an unpredictable woman. You never know which way she's going to go. One day you know nothing and you get a ten because she is happy; another day she gets off on the wrong side of the bed and she fails you even if you have studied and know a lot. Without the slightest hint as to what you did to deserve it.

And then there's Biochemisty. You started off very poorly: you got marked one on the written test. That means that if you want to pass, you have to get two tens.

But what happens in Biochemistry is totally different from what happens in other subjects. The whole area is messy and boring. Incomprehensible. You have had enough of Mendeleieff and you have diagrams with letters and drawings up to your ears. But then, there is Miss Bernardini, who is sensational to say the least. So, so good... we are talking movie star material. She has something you used to like a lot about Marcela: that sexy voice, and the way she moves and laughs when you say something stupid. She also has something that reminds you of Ava Gardner which you cannot define. Maybe it is the combination of her dark hair and those green almond eyes. Maybe the way she sounds so mature, so experienced. Miss Bernardini, like Estrada, sometimes gives you the feeling she's just another friend.

The only thing that bothers you is that you cannot communicate with her very well. She lives in a scientific world where you're a foreigner. A totally illiterate foreigner. By now you have learnt that there are people who don't like what you like, people who don't like you, whatever you do, and that there are people who like you even if you don't like them.

But you have some special moments with Miss Bernardini. You know she likes you and you like her, in spite of that huge chasm that exists between the things a humanist likes (because you already consider yourself a humanist) and what a scientist likes. So there are times when you shoot the breeze with her during breaks and she kind of accepts you talking to her and she even smiles and everything.

The Literature hour is over. It was really easy because you and Jorge talked about French movies with Estrada and he ended up forgetting about *Calderón de la Barca*. The rest of the kids were very grateful for the distraction.

And Duval's hour is also over. She was talking about something, you don't even remember. Now all you have left are loose words like '*Gestalt*' and '*cognitive*' and you also remember how everybody laughed when Dr Duval explained that Woodworth had said something about schools of psychology in 1931 and Raúl had asked 'He said that what is what?'.

The bell rings and you have that oppressive certainty that come the end of the break the hour of truth will be upon you, because it is quite possible that Miss Bernardini may tell you to come to the platform and talk—and maybe write something on the blackboard—about aliphatic compounds and the Maxwell-Boltzmann Law. It's also quite possible that she may give you a mark much lower than ten, because you know absolutely nothing about aliphates or Maxwell and Co.

Having to sit the test in Biochemistry would be quite possibly the nightmare from which you cannot escape. If she fails you, forget about uni for ever and ever.

You have to do something. If you don't strike first, it may cost you your life. Your mum always says that, if you don't talk, people are not going to guess what you want.

"Miss, I need to talk to you now."

"What... right now? Now we have to talk about aliphatic compounds and salts."— the words are like empty shells, they don't make the slightest sense. The only word that stays in your mind is the word 'now'.

"Yes, right now, if at all possible. (Is that you saying that?)"

"Let's see... wait a bit ..."—she turns around to talk to the rest of the class and you are so close that you can almost visualise the perfume she's wearing, and your hormones go into orbit just by brushing against the *Banlon*® outfit she's got on. "OK, kids, start writing about anything you can remember on the last three points we saw this week. This is not a test, but in about ten minutes I will ask you about what you wrote, OK?"

When she finishes talking to the others and turns towards you, you're on your own, right in front of her, about one centimetre away from her, fighting against the aroma of that bloody *Intimate*, that pervades your senses; the fear of failing Biochemistry, which is like the Four Horsemen of the Apocalypse galloping behind you; the hormones, that continue on their trip towards some orbit somewhere; and your cheeks, assuming a deep vermilion colour which you can feel beneath your skin, very warm, like coming back from the beach.

"Let's see, Campos, what did you have to tell me that was so important?"

"Well... anyway, I'm not sure how to start."

"How about you start from the beginning?"

"Well, you know that I really like you perhaps as much as I dislike Biochemistry..."

"I don't understand what you're trying to tell me."

"... I know I can be candid with you and that you will understand me. Thing is we both know that the moment I leave school, whatever I end up doing, I will never use Biochemistry anywhere else, so whatever I learn here is going to be totally irrelevant in my life."

"Why? What are you going to do?"

"I'm going to write, of course."

"And what are you going to write?"

"So far what I do is poems and some pieces of prose. It's all a bit incoherent and a bit for my own use, but I will do it professionally."

"That sounds excellent. And what do you want me to do?"

"I have to get two tens to pass the subject. All I need is a chance to do it."

"Look, Campos, I'm not promising anything, but let's do a deal: you bring me the things you have been writing. I would really like to see your poems. I will read them. If I see you have what it takes to be an author, I will give you topics for two special classes. But you have to prepare them really well, OK?" — While she says 'OK' you analyse her lips, her cheeks, that spot she has near her mouth… and you ask yourself if that look in her huge green eyes is maternal or what. Maybe she feels sorry for you. Anyway, main thing is that you're in with a chance.

"OK. On Thursday I'll bring something for you to read."

JORGE'S JAW has not touched the floor, but it's much closer than normal. His eyes are wide open and round. He puts the sunglasses in the inner pocket of his jacket.

"You told her that?"—Jorge is walking backwards, ahead of you. He won't let you go through without an answer. His curiosity is killing him.

"And she agreed? You're *the* guy. That is pure genius. Tell me, what else did she say? Dude, you've got her. I'm putting money on the table."— (when Jorge gets going he can say some stupid things).

"You don't know what you're talking about. She told me she's going to give me a chance that I didn't have until now. Getting two tens without her help, with that shitty subject, would be more than a miracle."

"No, kid, listen to me. It's more than that. She's into you, believe me. Who would have known you could be charming, man."

"Stop the bullshit, will you? This is a very special arrangement, but it's strictly professional." The idea, however, flatters you so much that you cannot stop smiling.

∼

ON THURSDAY, one minute before the beginning of Biochemistry, you go to the front of the classroom and, silently, leave a green cardboard folder on the desk, gazing at Miss Bernardini's eyes. Afterwards, with sheer premeditation, you affect your best innocent face and pull a little withered flower out of your pocket, you dust it a bit with the other hand to get rid of any fluff, and you place it on the folder. The effect is quite theatrical. You turn around and go back to your seat. Silence. Miss Bernardini picks up folder and flower and puts them in her briefcase. During class, you and she continue with your best poker faces, as if nothing had happened. You remember your mum and the still waters, an abyss in the middle of the ocean.

∼

ON MONDAY you cannot wait for Tuesday. On Tuesday you wait for the Biochemistry hour. It seems quite incredible, but you're waiting for it. What actually happens is that you want to see her, doesn't matter what she says, whether she gives you a chance or not. You don't even care about sitting that fucking Biochemistry test.

The classroom is as noisy as usual. The door opens and she walks in with the books between her arm and that Greek goddess hip that she has. With the other hand she carries her briefcase. There is silence, which is what is supposed to happen when a teacher walks into the classroom. She leaves the briefcase on the desk and signals with her hand that those who are still standing should sit down. She starts talking about things you don't hear, because all that is normally your reality is now unreal. The rest of the kids take their folders from under their desks. All of a sudden, the green eyes look at you and smile:

"Campos, come here a moment, will you?"

You stand up and walk towards the platform like an automaton. The kids are already writing something that is a total mystery to you. The unreality becomes more unreal. The perfume shrouds your seventeen years like a thick fog. The green eyes are very close and the smile on her lips utters words that surround you even more.

"Did you understand? … What's wrong? You OK?"

"No, I went to bed very late last night, and on top of that I didn't sleep well; I don't know, nightmares and all that."

"… I was telling you that you write very well. I like it. I like it very much."—the smile has a softness, a shared intimacy thing about it, or maybe that's what you're reading in it. In any case, you even admit to yourself that you are in the middle of the most absurd crush ever.

"Look, here are your writings. I kept a page that I want to read again. There's no problem with the two special classes. But we cannot discuss them right now. What I propose is this: come to my place on Wednesday around seven thirty. I wrote the address and the phone number in the folder. So we can talk about what you write and I suggest the topics for your classes. And you choose the two you like best. What do you think?"

"Sounds good."

～

IMAGINE your friend Jorge's face during the break when you tell him: it goes from enthusiasm to extasy and then to the cool smile.

"Told you, kid: you've got her."

"Stop it, man. You have no idea what you're talking about... You're thinking about *Tea and Sympathy*. Movies are movies. This is real life. I know very well her tone when she talks to me."— (At that stage you know Jorge is right and you want to convince yourself nothing is happening because you're afraid of failure). "Nothing's happening. Why would she even look at me, tell me, with all the possibilities she has? She has guys around her like flies. I don't know, grown up men, with money, a car, and everything. I don't even have a fucking scooter. "

"Look, the only thing you have to promise me is that if anything happens, you tell me."—(In Jorge's mind, your triumph would the triumph of the student proletariat against the teaching oligarchy).

"Of course, No problem. In any case, nothing's going to happen."

～

AFTER ALL THE PREPARATIONS, after thinking it over two, three, four times. After having rehearsed fifty thousand times what you're going to say, you arrive at her house, wearing a blue blazer, your best necktie, new moccasins and a touch of *Aqua Velva Ice Blue* on your face (not too much, because there's nothing worse than too much perfume). The house is an old two-storey French cottage, with ivy covering the front wall and mossy slate roof. When you ring the bell you are very nervous, but all you think about is that you just want to see her. What's more amazing, and what you keep repeating to yourself, is that she's not a girl: she's a teacher, and you're not going on a date: you're going to see her about something to do with school. In any case, what you feel is very different.

When she opens the door, it's like a *Technicolor* movie (with the years you learn that those moments are rare and that, when you're living them, the only thing you can do is enjoy them intensely).

The smile. The gesture inviting you in. That voice that is so attractive. And those movements that are so self-assured and that flow so well all the time. Everything's perfect. You look at the living room, very *Provençal* and very elegant, and think about Jorge, teasing you. The thoughts go away almost immediately.

"Come in. Sit down. I was about to have a cup of coffee. Would you like one?" Her tone is very natural, but it doesn't sound even close to how she sounds in class. Maybe that's the way it seems to you, nothing else. She keeps on walking, to look for your cup of coffee.

"I would love one. Your house is so beautiful!" (Does she notice, that even when she's not looking at you, you cannot stop leering at her?).

"Ah, thank you, do you like it? Everything is exactly the way mum and dad left it. I'll bring some sweets too, if you like."— from the kitchen, her voice sounds echoey.

"Yes, thank you"— you raise your voice a bit— "Do you mind if I smoke?"

"No, light one for me too. Sometimes I like a smoke. You are Alberto, aren't you? Call me Susana, because we're not at school, OK?"

"OK."

You feel relieved. You are in control again. This is the final stretch and you're riding several lengths ahead. She's all yours. In your mind you can hear a *milonga* Carlitos Gardel used to sing. You can even hear the guitars some place near the nape of your neck: "...this race is mine, honey, I won it with my pony...".

She comes back from the kitchen. She places the tray on the coffee table and sits very close to you, knees together, pointing towards you.

"Well..."—for a fraction of a second, her tone of voice is that of the teacher, but it becomes immediately diluted into that other intimate tone that is so soothing— "maybe we should start with the special classes, but before that I want to tell you that your writing has something quite admirable about it. If you don't write you're going to waste it and you'll be wasting a very special talent. And the rest of us are going to miss out on that beautiful thing. I don't know what you'll be doing. Not sure if you're going to be a novelist, or a playwright, or what. But if what I ask you has any value to you, I ask you to devote yourself to that talent." — Both her hands—warm—take yours.

What follows should probably remain in your mind alone. That kiss stays, indelible, as the first kiss from a true woman. Susana's words and whispers, mixed with yours, still come back to you at night, or when you walk alone those evenings, after so many years.

"This is not going to happen again"—she tells you, placing her hand between your mouth and hers, and Deborah Kerr's image in *Tea and Sympathy* becomes superimposed onto Jorge's stupid smile for a fraction of a second— "... and it's not going to happen again, in the first place, because it should never have happened. But it is real because you and I want it to happen and because we need it. You're a beautiful human being and I feel that you're my little man, but in reality you're not. You belong to some girl who's going to turn up in your life. She's going to love you and follow you to the other side of the world, if necessary."—The palm of her hands join under your chin while they frame your face. And the green eyes smile very close to you. Her lips come closer and she kisses you again—"In any case, this moment is already yours and mine, forever."

JORGE, always at the ready, is leaning on the bookshop window. You approach him with a wide smile.

"Told you, man, back to reality. She gave me the topics, which is something amazing. Nothing else happened, though. But she's quite a woman, Susana."

"Ah, now you call her Susana. I knew something was going to happen."

"You're such an idiot, aren't you? You believe me every time."
— Jorge laughs, accepting the joke.

"Do you want to go to Palermo?"

"Let's go."

MONTHS LATER, your world has shifted; all you can think about is uni.

One day you see her passing while you wait for the bus to go to Lomas de Zamora. She's with a group of friends. From the distance, she smiles at you, intimately. Only you can understand that smile."

BIOCHEMISTRY *

$\mathcal{T}$he story is just that, a story. The names were changed, of course, to protect the innocent, and we were all innocent. It was written in 2010, as part of the festivities at the *Escuela Normal de Banfield* to celebrate the fiftieth anniversary of the high school class of 1960.

Other peculiarities of the narration are that, 1) it is a long monologue, a tirade of a middle-aged man that begins criticising the educational system in Australia and ends up telling his son about a love affair he had with his chemistry teacher and 2) it is a study of narration in second person singular.

Love stories, or infatuations, between teachers and students are not new. They have happened many times before and will keep on happening because that is part of human nature. We fall in love. Regardless of age.

In the 2006 British movie, *Notes on a Scandal*, starring Cate Blanchett, the scandal is exactly that, a teacher is discovered in a sexual encounter with a student. An older teacher, played by

Judi Dench, uses the affair to manipulate the main character into becoming her lover. Eventually the main character is sentenced to ten months gaol. In this case, the movie centers on the two women rather than on the sexual affair with the student.

Recently, there have been a few of those affairs in real life. The most spectacular, the most famous one, was that of Mary Kay Letourneau and Vili Fualaau, a sixth-grade teacher and her thirteen-year-old student. That happened towards the end of the century. Their illicit sexual relationship was reported to police and Mary Kay, who was already a mother of four, was sentenced to three months behind bars. At that point, she was not allowed to see Vili. There was another encounter while prohibited from seeing him and she then had to serve seven years in gaol.

On being released from prison, Vili and Mary Kay got married. Their marriage lasted 12 years and they had two daughters. She died in 2020, of cancer complications, when she was 58 years of age.

They considered each other "the love of their life". The unfortunate side of the story was that Mary Kay was registered as a paedophile (which she undoubtedly had become after Vili) even though she had no prior history of paedophilia.

In our story, in Alberto and Susana's case, it is just one encounter. One beautiful encounter in *Technicolor*, nothing else. Nevertheless, let me emphasise one last thing: I passed biochemistry.

DIFFERENT REALITIES IN AN
ABSENT OLD AGE

*- To Anni,
for her generous help.*

*"Day was dawning: light suffused the room... I thought fearfully,
'Where am I?' and I realised I didn't know. I thought, 'Who am I?'
and I couldn't recognise myself. My fear grew. I thought: This
desolate awakening is hell, this eternal vigil will be my destiny."*
- Jorge Luis Borges

*H*e climbed the steps two at a time. The staircase was in semi-twilight; the handrail shone a mahogany darkness. That's how his work was. The usual thing: he had to go from one end to the building to the other. Somebody had ordered that the closest door to the Senate had to stay closed. So he had to go around.

He passed the office of the Secretary of the House of Reps.

"Good morning, Pintos." – The orderly was shining something and said it without even turning his head.

"Good morning."

There was a long corridor ahead of him. The floor tiles, with their typical design, kept on appearing as he walked. Light was coming from the courtyard, dim and casual. The sole of his left shoe squeaked obstinately, in spite of the rain.

The decree was already late for the Senate. He passed the Library, in a hurry. From the Grand Hall he could glimpse *Pasos Perdidos* at the other side of the building. He kept going. The Senate, with its hallways and secret corridors was, in his mind, much more than a beautiful labyrinth. In the Senate, his father's presence followed him, like an invisible cloak, everywhere.

He left the file with the decree on the employee's desk.

"Kid, Is this for the Secretary?

"No, it's for for Carlitos Gardel". – That 'kid' thing had bothered him. He had been ten years in Parliament House. He was the Secretary of the *Dirección de Ayuda Social*. People in the House of Reps knew him. He did understand, however, that the Senate was a different world.

He turned around as he was leaving.

"Ah, and he wants it *right now*".

CALLAO AVENUE TILES, broken as usual, played at being new again: they would shine with every drop. He crossed the street holding his raincoat's collar. Rain and everything, the walk to his flat in Lavalle and Paraná held endless surprises. Corrientes was a fiesta of bookshops and cinemas. Reaching the flat he looked at the central heating. It had never worked. He had to buy a heater. After hanging his jacket in the wardrobe he went to sleep thinking about Saturday's French movie: Anouk Aimee.

~

HE PEEPED with one eye without understanding much. He slowly opened the other eye. It didn't help either.

He was in a house. Whose house would that be? Would it be his? Who was that woman sleeping next to him? Was she his wife? All those things around him were vaguely familiar but they had something strange about them he couldn't explain.

Inés, half asleep, stretched her hand in a warm caress. Time returned gradually, free from all metaphor: twenty-six years of marriage, the house on the Gold Coast. He was himself. He was a translator. Many trips. Much life together with her.

He explained to Inés what had happened and they laughed about it. They felt the absence had been somewhat funny. Being without having been. Not knowing. Not understanding what was what. The episode remained in the back of his mind as something unimportant.

~

THAT WEEK he had planned a trip to Melbourne. Things happened unhurriedly until he found himself at Coolangatta airport. The flight, the flight attendants. Zoe, who went to pick him up. His son, Rodrigo; chats, and the trip to Sorrento.

The summer house. That tranquil setting of the bay. They dined at a nearby pizza place.

The sun was beginning to come through the window. He woke up alone in an unknown bedroom. There was an oar on the wall and other nautical allusions. But nothing revealed to him what was what.

Where was he? Who was he? Petrified, he got up and walked through an undiscovered corridor. Dante had not even begun to imagine something like the abstraction that represents a date, he thought. A space without a name. A universe, real but unknown. Hell, he reminded himself, included more than Count Ugolino devouring his sons. The desperation—that somewhat timeless desperation—dissipated as he reached the end of the hallway. That was the moment he understood he was in Sorrento. He slowly discovered that existing in Victoria was a possibility.

THEY WALKED through Banfield talking such nonsense. Politics, literature, girls, cinema: everything had to be mixed with the continuous jokes that are part and parcel of being young. Banfield was the world they knew. Alem street would take them from Leblón—which was the place to be seen in Lomas—to the Munich pub, across the road from Banfield railway station. Cortázar and Wilde would walk with them and would give their opinion, deep sometimes, witty, some other times. Spinoza, a bit darker, would follow them a few steps behind, putting some order in the universe. Was there another way to live? Juan used to hide his fears behind an intelligence and a culture that had been precocious some time ago. Where was the future? Ernesto, who understood everything the way it was meant to be understood, would talk about women.

Argentina, with its political and economic comings and goings, continued making normal life impossible, at least the way he imagined it. Somebody had said "Living is possible but they don't let you". It was true. The only way out—tautological as it was—involved leaving. Juan's vain and medieval warnings were that the Atlantic led nowhere and that when you reached the edge you would fall.

That night he reached the flat, via an almost empty car of the Roca line of the railways. *Constitución* Station and the subway. He went to bed slowly. Buenos Aires ended mixed up with his oneiric town. His aunt Chile's winter garden. A never ending party, eternal, countless times repeated, with people he didn't know. He went to the balcony, where he could see Meeks Avenue in the darkness. He left without talking to anybody. And without talking to anybody he walked through the vaulted arcades, with their brick statues, and the gloomy red church. He crossed the bridge and reached the street that came down from the hill, where the Portuguese and the Vietnamese would come from. There was no more logic and he knew it. The subconscious reigned, all alone.

HE HAD A SHOWER. Next thing he knew, he was leaning on the wardrobe door. Didn't understand what was going on; why things were the way the were, everything in such a mess. Inés explained, repeatedly: the carpet people were coming to change the bedroom carpets. He gradually understood that present, again.

The episodes grew exponentially, dramatically, again and again. He felt that his absences—still distant and unfathomable —were almost poetical.

The neurologist explained that there were connections in his brain that sometimes were unsuccessful. It was an illness of the soul that required medication for the brain. He accepted it without saying a word. He then understood that all his past had been a dream. Time and space did not exist. Reality existed only in the present. Old age, Offenbach, and his birds.

ABOUT WRITING *

Working on this book I discovered that authors are a rather immodest bunch. Their vocation involves disrobing unashamedly in front of the world.

An actor wears a mask. Authors, even when they write fiction, are willing to display some degree of nakedness.

It is not all showing off.

In their effort to communicate, they have to choose the ultimate vulnerability. Directly or indirectly, it feels as if they must tell everybody else not only what they think but probably how they think as well.

NOTES

5. BORGES AND THE BOOK OF SAND *

1. The Spanish language versions of this story, *Wilson*, and its accompanying segment, *Borges and the Book of Sand*, were respectively published in the March 2018 and June 2019 editions of *Encuentros en Recoleta*, an eMagazine in Buenos Aires.

6. A CONSPIRACY AGAINST TIME

1. The Spanish language version of this short story was published in a literary magazine in the year 2000, in Europe, as *Evidencia de una conspiración contra el tiempo – Documento probatorio "A", Revista Abril, January 2000, Luxembourg.*

ACKNOWLEDGMENTS

I am indebted to Inés, who has demonstrated that some wives are endowed with unimaginable stocks of love and understanding. She gave me all the support I needed to finish this book.

I also want to thank Zoe McKenzie, a political consultant who happens to be my daughter-in-law. Zoe read and edited the stories and provided great advice and information throughout the process.

John Watts gave me detailed and useful tips, read and commented each and every story. A career diplomat, John was in Japan, in the middle of the pandemic, and still found the time to help me with the book.

どうもありがとうございました.

I am grateful to all three.